JABALI ISLAND

EDDIE GENEROUS

JABALI ISLAND

WWW.SEVEREDPRESS.COM

ISBN: 978-1-922861-97-9

1

The sand was mucky underfoot, the moonlight reflecting against the wet edges of a newly dug gutter that trailed around one of the resort's numerous gazebos. All of the woodwork at the resort was so fresh it still harbored that earthy lumber scent. Though, now, there was something heavier on the air.

"She went this way?" Charli Crook said as she stepped next to the wet gulley cut into the white, white sand.

"Think so. She went off with Mr. Abs," Susan Marshall said.

Susan was Charli's half-sister; unlike Charli, she hadn't changed her name, hadn't had a boob job, and had 137 Instagram followers. Charli had more than 30 million, as of that morning.

"Totes her," Charli pulled out her phone. "Hmm? No selfies with him after leaving. Nodda on posts at all; totes *not* her."

They were on the search for a friend of Charli's, another influencer. In fact, Summer Dallas was the reason they were there. She'd been invited to opening night at the resort, a resort so far from civilization only one plane had clearance to land. The South Pacific, just about equal distance both ways between New Zealand and Chile, surrounded Jabali Island.

"Why are we chasing her down?" Susan said, then, almost absently, added, "What do you think was dragged here?"

"Probably a drunk guest."

They had passed two gazebos and were getting close to the forest. Most of the island was forest, or volcano. Prior to building the resort, only locals of nearby islands ever visited, for hunting purposes. Sometime, likely within the last five or six hundred years, these hunters had visited, and perhaps explorers had as well, given the make up of the place in 2023. Whether it was intentional or not, they'd left animals, animals that eventually thrived on the plentiful local flora, possibly even some of the visiting avian wildlife.

"Something weird about this. It's not water," Susan said, crouched and leaning close to the sand gulley.

Susan stalled their search to pull her cellphone from the back pocket of her tiny white jeans—Charli had dressed her; if Susan was going to *assist* her the week they were on the island, it damned well better not look badly upon her. The shine hit the dark, sandy liquid. It looked black beneath the blue light. And thick.

"I think it's blood."

Charli scoffed. "Girl, you need to lay off the true crime podcasts."

"No, for real." Susan reached with a timid finger and touched the bottom of the gulley.

"Eww," Charli said, then turned her phone and snapped thirteen photos of herself with the ocean in the background in the matter of a few seconds. The flash was brilliant on the dark beach.

Susan was about to say that *she really, really thought it was blood*—the stuff was definitely red on her fingertip—but a series of loud snaps silenced her. Both women looked to the black wall of trees, only the fronds at the tops visible in the moonlight. Those fronds shook gently.

"What's that?" Charli whispered.

"Let's go back," Susan whispered in return.

"What if it's Summer?" Charli whispered, then called out, "Summer, that you?"

The rustling ceased. Susan shined her flashlight on the trees, then on everything between them and the trees, and when nothing presented itself, she scanned it all once more. Next to the gulley was a dead pelican, its chest gaping and red beneath the blue light. Its dead eyes looked sugar-coated, the sand almost white.

"Eww, gross," Charli said, her tone expressing honest offense. "They need better cleaners. I shouldn't have to look at that."

"It's the middle of the night?" Susan said, shifting her light back to the forest.

"Doesn't matter. This resort wants to impress me and my following with dead birds on the beach? Probably, Summer saw the bird and ran inside." All whispering and caution gone; there was no room for either alongside her outrage. "I should Insta the bird. Show these lazy bums people need to actually work around here."

Susan blinked rapidly. Her half-sister had always had it easy, relying on her beauty and natural physical attributes—then, once she could afford them, silicone attributes. She'd never had a real job in her life. Susan, being the opposite, had had many jobs but hadn't been able to keep any of them. And she worked hard. Nights, when her mind refused her the sleep she needed, she wondered if Charli had somehow extracted the good luck due to Susan, then applied it to herself.

"Let's go back," Susan said, shifting her light to Charli.

Charli's face was awash in the ambient glow of her iPhone. "Fine," she said.

Susan exited from the flashlight app—she was already hovering around 39% battery—and pocketed the device. She turned to head back, the lights of the resort bright, despite their goodly distance from where she stood.

A rattle of branches crackled. Growls and snorts overshadowed the gentle South Pacific lapping. Charli screamed as the noises grew in strength, drew nearer in proximity.

Susan spun, wide-eyed. Charli was not where she had been. Susan fiddled with her phone, fingers suddenly all but useless. She got the flashlight app lit. She found a fresh gulley, not as bloody as the last, but bloody nonetheless.

"Susan?" Charli said, her voice small, small, small.

Susan shined the light closer to the forest and found her half-sister, her body hidden behind a palm frond. "Charli, are you—" She took three racing steps, stopping at the thumping grunting sounds that jerked Charli's head and shoulders—

something had her beyond sight. “Charli?” Susan whined.

The grunting, snorting sounds deepened. Charli rocked harder, a gush of blood firing up her throat. Susan shook all over, stepping backward.

“I’ll get help. It’ll be okay.”

A moment before sprinting away, Susan heard the unmistakable sounds of lapped liquid and the chewing of meat. Tears spilled down her cheeks and a whine played steadily up her throat as she burned along the beach, racing for the light and suggested safety of the resort. She had no clue what kind of animal could do that and had an off-putting idea that whether she wanted it or not, she’d find out before the night was through.

2

Jumbo Joe Bourque had his hand out, showing off the huge cup ring he'd finally won after seventeen years playing pro hockey. Come this most recent off-season, he wasn't quite ready to retire, but his agent called and informed him he didn't have any choice…unless he wanted to play in Europe for a pittance. If he was being honest with himself, he had to admit that his cardio wasn't where it had been, his scorer's touch was gone, and teams these days simply didn't need multiple enforcers—a role he'd begrudgingly stepped into after the other skills began to slip because he threw fists that felt like iron and had a head built of similar stuff. Enforcers were cheap and plentiful, and many of the young ones kept up to the pace of play well enough to keep from being defensive liabilities. His squad didn't want him and none of the thirty-one other GMs his agent had called wanted him either.

"Must've been some relief, huh?" a young man said, dancing to the salsa-rap thumping through the speakers in the resort's hall—a glitzy space about half the size of a pro-basketball court, minus the seats.

"Some relief to get on a team that would carry him to a cup you mean?" another man said, this one not as young, though trying his damndest to look it.

Jumbo Joe smirked. He was 6'4" and 240 pounds, built like a slab of concrete—aside from the little bit of flab that had settled over a six-pack that was now a thing of memories. He'd taken the job as security supervisor because the resort wanted him, and were willing to pay him the kind of cash that had him swallowing his pride. He was a gimmick, he understood that, but he wasn't about to play because everyone on the island, aside from the help, were multi-millionaires. If he'd been smarter about it, he would've stashed a hell of a lot more than three million—he'd made more than double that, take home, some seasons. Of course, he'd earned every penny he ever blew at a table, invested stupidly, or donated when needing a PR lift.

"That's pretty good," Jumbo Joe said. "Let me guess, you're an Oilers fan. Mad at me for knocking them out in oh-seven."

The older-trying-to-look-young man sneered. "What?"

"You going to pretend you don't remember that? Going to pretend you're not a Millennial?"

The younger one looked to the older one, smirking. "Is that why you don't have your birthday anywhere online?"

"I don't care how tough you think—hey!"

Jumbo Joe scooped the man up, one hand on his shoulder and the other on his thigh. "What's that?" he said. "I can't hear you, have to wait for a break in play."

"Put me down!"

A crowd quickly gathered. Jumbo Joe knew it might cost him his overpaying job, but as he'd done, for better or worse, through his adult life, he followed his gut and did what felt right. He shifted the man's weight. His left hand came down; now the man was on a single arm like art atop a pedestal.

"I'll sue you and—Ah!"

Jumbo Joe started to bounce and spin the man on one massive hand. The crowd began clapping. The DJ caught on quickly and Outkast's *Hey Ya* filled the room. The fun and enthusiasm filled Jumbo Joe with energy and purpose. He so hated generational wealth and the turds it produced.

"I'll have your job! Let me down!"

Jumbo Joe, arm tired now, said, "Sure," and turned slightly to let the man drop about five feet to a vacant dining table.

The man popped up and charged at Jumbo Joe, a traumatized and furious expression on his face. He reached up to put a finger in the big man's face.

"You'll be in jail for that. My dad's the best lawyer in—oww!"

Grinning, Jumbo Joe had the man's finger and was twisting it. The man tried to twist with it. "Hardly a crime out here…I mean, I'm as close to a cop as this island has."

"Please, let go," the man said, whining, finally achieving the aura of someone much younger. "It hurts."

Jumbo Joe looked around, recognizing that nobody was smiling now and he knew he looked like a bully rather than a champion of righteous comeuppance. He let go.

The man stumbled back, his expression suggesting he might come for more, but he ultimately disappeared through the crowd. Jumbo Joe waved his arms at the natural and unnatural beauties surrounding him, a good number of which had their phones out.

Likely it was too late now. Jumbo Joe laughed inwardly. He'd be looking for a new job by tomorrow…maybe. The world had become awfully confusing in the last ten years or so—a stark difference from his youth shoveling shit, shooting pigeons, and bringing in crops on the farm in Northern Saskatchewan. If his little stunt made the resort trend long enough, his boss might give him a bonus instead of canning him for abusing guests.

"All right, show's over, the play's over yonder now," Jumbo Joe said, waving at the many cellphones gripped in manicured hands.

A woman came running into the room, makeup raccooning her face. Her eyes were wide, her mouth open. She looked wild, tripping perhaps. Jumbo Joe started toward her in a jog. Minding this woman was his job, and right now he'd take any distraction from thinking about what tomorrow might bring.

3

"He said he was going to be here at ten on the dot, his words, 'on the dot,'" Benoit Zary said to two other concierges in on the deal.

They were to meet up with the man named Q by the hot springs at 10:00 PM. The investors behind the resort had a policy concerning drugs: they didn't want to see them, didn't want to hear about them, couldn't supply them, but they had to be on the island. *Had to be*. Benoit figured that was hardly an issue—was sure the other concierges, waitstaff, and various entertainers wouldn't be offended either. Of those he'd asked, all had been plucked from escort services, including himself. Hot people willing to pleasure guests without tipping them off that they were professionals until after the fact sounded like smart business.

Footfalls approached along the path. The trio turned to look, matching flashlight beams falling on a tall woman with hair the color of corn silk. Her arms were shapely with muscle, her shoulders broad. She looked to be somewhere between fifty and seventy—a good plastic surgeon made it impossible to tell for sure these days.

Benoit put on a sly smile that had almost always worked with women of a certain age in the past. "Can I help you, miss?" he said—never ma'am, anything but ma'am to this breed of women…unless they demanded it.

"'Miss,' that's cute," the woman said, accent thick, posh British. "I don't think so, I'm just out for a walk. Was hoping to get a look from a view I saw online."

Benoit stepped closer. "Let me guess: a night shot from a natural lookout, moon seemingly ready to dip into the volcano like it was a biscuit and the volcano a cup of tea."

The woman laughed. "Yes, that's correct."

"Perhaps you'd like a guide?" Benoit said, slipping his hands into the pockets of his loose pants in a way that spread his shirt, putting a flat tummy on display.

"I'd love one…I'm Mary Aterton, by the way." The woman held out her hand.

"Benoit Groulx." He lifted her hand as he bent forward, kissing a knuckle, inadvertently taking stock of the diamonds in a ring and bracelet.

Mary tittered.

"Permit me a moment to speak to my cohorts before I run off, hmm?" Benoit said.

Mary waved him away and he hurried to the other concierges, stepping in tight enough that his whisper would reach only his intended targets.

"Stay here to wait for Q. If he doesn't show inside an hour, see if you can't find him back at the hotel," Benoit said. "It's possible he's jet lagged or operating in the wrong time zone."

The others nodded. Benoit hurried to Mary's side.

"Shall we?" Benoit said, holding out an arm.

Mary accepted. "Certainly. Is it far?"

They began walking.

"A little ways, but I promise to be as agreeable as possible."

"Of course you do."

Benoit led them back, almost to where the main light of the resort touched, but not quite. Instead, they walked with linked arms down another path, small solar lights every five feet along the way, their glow moody and romantic.

"Tell me about yourself," Benoit said.

"Okay, why not?" Mary said, then got onto the topic of herself: grew up on the happier side of the middle-class, married young, divorced in her forties into massive wealth, started and ran a designer purse, watch, underwear empire until last year, had no children, and only came to the resort on a lark. "Bit absurd, having a resort way out here."

Benoit shrugged. "As long as the check clears, I can handle being here for four months."

Jabali Island had four months of all but guaranteed nice weather, the other eight kept the island beneath a shroud of either rain or migrating insects, dependent on the month.

The lookout was a little over two miles from the resort proper. It featured a bench, a steel, animal-resistant garbage can, and the same kind of solar lights that had lit the path. The grass was kept short, though little had been done by way of landscaping otherwise. Uneven with large stones jutting roughly, the lookout offered a bit of both worlds, perhaps leaning closer to wilderness thanks to the thick forest bordering two sides.

Mary sat down on the bench and looked across the drop off to the volcano about three miles away. Benoit sat down next to her. The moon was high, killing the dunking biscuit effect.

"Tell me, Benoit, are you a gigolo?"

He didn't look at her. "I'm a concierge, but I'm not averse to plying a trade I've nearly perfected."

Mary clicked her tongue. "Perfected, huh? I suppose we'll have to put that to the test."

"As you wish," Benoit said, rising and taking Mary's hand to stand her up. "Can it wait, or shall we find a nice patch of grass?"

"Certainly it can wait, but I'd prefer we find a nice patch of grass," Mary said, her tummy pressed against Benoit's, their lips nearly touching.

Benoit remedied the disconnection, slipping his tongue into her mouth the moment their lips came together. His hands played to the small of her back, then pulled her tight to him. Neither acknowledged the snapping of tree limbs in the woods not far from the clearing as they walked clumsily toward a smooth patch of grass that sat in a strip of moonlight.

4

Jumbo Joe pulled Susan out of the busy, boisterous dance hall and into the lobby of the hotel. A couple leaned against a wall by the coatroom, hands roaming, mouths pressed together. Jumbo Joe led the harried and stiff-legged Susan to a leather couch next to a massive fireplace with four glass walls.

"Something happened to your friend, you said?" Jumbo Joe said, leaning in close, trying to be personable.

She kept her face down, shaking her head gently, then nodding. "There's an animal…I think."

"You think?"

Susan sighed, swiping at her nose. "I didn't see it. We went out looking for Charli's friend Summer. There's a trench in the sand, and there's blood in it. We followed it, sort of. We started just walking down the beach because Summer told—"

"Maybe get to what happened?" Jumbo Joe said, not unkindly. "If time is of the essence…you know."

Susan finally looked him in the eyes. He was leaning low, to her level—he had about ten inches on her. "Right. Well, we got pretty near the forest and when we were about to give up on Summer and come back, something dragged Charli away. I didn't see what did it, but I saw her…I saw her die. It was thumping and shaking her, but I couldn't see what it was. It killed her, I'm sure of it!"

The couple quit fooling around long enough to stare at Jumbo Joe and Susan. Jumbo Joe straightened and folded his arms across his chest. "Can I help you?" he said to the couple.

The couple looked away instantly. Within seconds, they were crossing the lobby toward the stairs to the rooms.

"Okay, then what?"

Susan put her hands palms up. "Then I ran back here for help."

Jumbo Joe frowned. "If you didn't check her vitals, maybe she's not dead?" He wasn't trying to sound condescending, but this was a lot for his first day on the job, especially since he was no more than a figurehead—and might get fired by morning for spinning a millionaire's kid like pizza dough. "Would you be willing to take me to where you left her? Really ought to see this through a hundred and ten percent."

Susan's expression tensed and her eyes widened. "Maybe if you bring a big gun."

Jumbo Joe pouted out his bottom lip in thought. "If there is a predatory animal, probably be better off with a little offensive firepower, sure."

"Okay," Susan said.

"You wait here." Jumbo Joe pushed to his feet, both knees crunching like he'd stashed Corn Flakes behind his kneecaps, and headed toward an office door behind the currently unmanned check-in desk. He pulled his phone from his pocket and sent a text to the man who really should've been in charge, since he had experience: *Gone down beach. Animal attack possibly.* He then opened the notepad on his phone to read the code he'd need to open the gun cabinet.

There were three rifles and two handguns inside. It was doubtful they'd need more than that. A box of cartridges went into his pocket. He took one of the rifles—a Franchi .308—and headed back to the lobby.

"I tried to text Summer; she still isn't answering. She's a phone junky, just like Charli," Susan said, then looked up. "What if that's not enough?"

Jumbo Joe's forehead became rolling waves as his eyebrows rose in surprise. "This would take down a grizzly, if shot close enough. Hell, probably could put a hole through an engine block and out the other side if fired close enough."

Susan shrugged at this.

5

Joey and Connor waited until Benoit and the woman left, and then some, before they started bitching about this Q figure they'd never met. Though they were paid well, they didn't earn any tips out in the woods, and despite being dumb as rocks—both of them—they were geniuses when it came to easing big tips out of lonely women.

"I been looking at getting into time shares," Joey said. He was a tall man, slender, with perfectly proportioned features. "Go on dates on beaches with all the women coming and going while I'm sitting pretty, work when I wanna, don't work when—"

"Wait, you gonna buy into a time share?" Connor was a shade under six feet, was top heavy with muscle, and had hair down to his shoulders, which he tied in a bun at the back of his head. "How you gonna get dates when you're only there for like two weeks a year?"

Joey tapped his temple—an act barely visible with only spotty moonlight shining down and the subtle glow from the path marker lights. "Gonna go in with a whole bunch of guys, you know? We get like twelve guys, each spend a month raking in dough in like Mexico or something, but then get to come back to the real world where it'll be easy living thanks to all the dates at the time share."

Connor scrunched his face. "That's kind of genius. Be like a whorehouse, but different."

Joey pointed, wide-eyed. "That's right. A whorehouse but different. After clearing what I will here, I figure I'll have like twenty-five grand saved up."

"Whoa, for real? Costs me just about all I can get from working to keep up with the shots."

"Shots?"

Connor danced his pecks beneath his tight Hugo Boss oxford that was part of the uniform. "I use this cocktail. It's like HGH and testosterone and other stuff. I heard it's the same mix the Liver King was using."

"Oh, yeah, that guy got wicked famous. I was thinking about getting all bulked up."

Connor smiled. "Yeah, man, I can train you in the gym they got here. It's pretty cool, doesn't have huge weights, but you don't really need huge weights. In fact, sometimes you can look pretty dumb when you're real big and you try real big weights in front of people. The shots, they're mostly for making you look big."

"Yeah? I had a buddy who got collagen in his chest and arms and—"

A thick tree branch snapped to their right. Both men turned their flashlights in that direction. The forest was still for one, two, three, five, ten seconds before another branch snapped, this one much closer than the last.

"Q? Is that you?" Connor called out, walking to the edge of the path.

Joey stepped up next to his compadre. "Hey, Q?"

The men shined their flashlights into the deep woods. It was all black lines and impenetrable shadows until Joey's beam locked onto a reflective eyeshine. Whatever it was out there, it appeared to stand about stomach high.

"What's that?" Joey said.

Connor's flashlight beam jerked to where Joey shined his. "Eyes."

"Yeah, but—look, two more."

Connor began waving his arm, nibbling at the thick darkness, finding two more sets of eyes. "Not raccoons. What kind of animals live on islands out here?"

Joey laughed a little. "You know, I bet it's a bunch of tortoises or something like that."

"Cool. Come here. Pssp, pssp, pssp."

Joey laughed a little more. "They're not cats."

"Well, I don't know. I never called a tortoise before."

Two by two, the eyes winked out, disappearing into the thick gloom. The men stood still for a ten count before Joey moaned in disappointment.

"Yeah, I thought they might come out," Connor said. "Maybe we can get them familiar, like as the days go by."

"But where the hell is—"

To their left, at the end of the path, branches snapped in a machine gun clatter. Both men jerked around, shining their beams on the massive bodies, pink with black spots. Neither saw a face until huge teeth were digging into their thighs.

“Pigs!” Joey shouted from the ground, two massive beasts over him, then pressing hooves into him as they rooted through his shirt, then his flesh. “Help!”

Connor was on his feet still, backpedaling, a large pig, hooves in his hands like they were dancing. A fourth pig bolted from the trees, nailing Connor in the back of the legs. He fell and the pig he’d been dancing with landed with most of its weight on the man’s chest.

“Ooog,” he moaned and began swinging.

Joey was all out of words and down to his last few breaths as the pigs attacking him had rooted open his ribcage and stomach and were about to feast on his soft, soft organs.

They were through the skin and tearing at muscles with Connor now, too. Connor roared before taking a great hooking swing at one of the pigs. His fist connected with a fantastic crunch. Bone and lumpy grey fluid oozed free around his fist, which remained lodged in the pig’s skull, while the pig continued munching. He jerked his fist free, depleting much of his quickly draining energy. His fist was covered in that nasty grey muck and bits of white bone.

“What kind of pigs…” Connor trailed, making eye-contact with a creature snout-deep beneath his breast plate.

Its eyes were a cataract’s cloudy off-white, emotionless and yet driven.

6

Mary sighed once the throbbing passed and Benoit ceased his thrusts. He gave her a quick kiss, then rolled off to deal with the condom. He stood naked beneath the moonlight, stretching as if he'd just awoken.

"You really are a pro, huh?" Mary said.

"I aim to please," Benoit said.

Mary gathered up her panties and bra. Benoit remained naked, posing now like a superhero awaiting a call from a shrieking damsel.

"So, how does this work?" Mary said, back in her dress, slipping her feet into her leather sandals. "Do you charge it to the room, or is this, what is this?"

"The companionship is covered, but any tips are greatly appreciated. And, of course, I can be available many more times throughout your stay."

Mary flushed. "Oh, right, maybe don't approach me in front of…I don't mean to sound…it's not you, it's just…"

Benoit smiled, his white, white teeth like bicycle reflectors beneath the moonlight. "I fully understand. Discretion is half the fun."

Mary, flustered, flipped her arms up above her head in a wave. "What even am I worrying about?"

Benoit took a step toward her. "There's nothing to worry about here. It's paradise."

A snorting, growling hum played out of the

forest. In a blink, two massive pigs—they had to weigh at least 2,000 pounds each—burst into the clearing, both aiming at Benoit's naked flesh. His eyes went wide and he did jazz hands at the creatures—the only defense he had. One pig bit his hand, jerking it back and forward. The other pig took hold of his genitals and in a blink, Benoit lost the most important facet of his income. He screamed, high and crazed.

Mary stumbled in reverse. "Hogs?" she said, then took two long strides back along the path. From the trees, another pig appeared. She had a moment to really drink in its bodily sum. This was no normal animal, and in fact, its smoothness and facial features made it look more like an oversized piglet than a full-grown hog…but the size of it!

Snorting and huffing, the pig sprinted toward her.

Benoit was on the ground, face down. A pig had its snout between his thighs, digging at the wound, while the other was on his back. His face was blank, his gaze pinned to his handless wrist and the rough chew marks that had torn his flesh and left the bones like splintered wood.

"Help! Somebody!" Mary shouted as she ran toward the cliff edge of the lookout.

The pig was gaining on her. No time to think, she reached the edge, then launched herself over. The pig followed her, stumbling on its little legs. Mary soared momentarily before plummeting down into a sea of fronds. They slapped as branches thumped heavily against her. The pig got no more than a foot from the edge before it tumbled against jagged rocks, its skull caving inward, sending out a great grey gush of chunky fluid.

Mary slammed on a branch that didn't break beneath her. The air was forced from her lungs; she whooped and gasped, moaning at the incredible pain of it, but her instincts kept her grip firm.

The pig reached the bottom, kicking and twitching. Its eyeballs dangled on either side of its ruined snout, below its flattened cranium. It attempted to rise, swinging its body. In the effort, what remained of its brain sloshed and slipped out of the ruined skull, detaching at the stem. It was grey, spotted with fuzzy growths.

The pig moved not an inch after the disconnection.

Nor did Mary move, aside from harsh breaths and the tears slipping down her face to the forest floor not so far below. She kept her eyes closed and her arms and legs wrapped tightly around the thick branch. There were no thoughts of a savior, no thoughts of finding a good place to hide, there were no thoughts at all, beyond clinging to that branch, despite how much it hurt to do so.

If she had to, Mary would wait out the end of time; the anxiety the danger and shock produced were just too much.

7

Jumbo Joe had been ready to disbelieve Susan from the moment she started speaking—no telling what kind of games a mind might play given the bottomless cups and assumed river of illicit substances that flowed at resorts—but the carved gulley was there, as was the blood. The blood had dried, the sand soaking it up like piss in a litter box. Getting to know her, albeit briefly, Susan also didn't seem like the uppity fare he'd observed since arriving. She was so human it made him wonder about her.

"Say, you a Canadian?" Jumbo Joe said.

Frowning, Susan leaned in close to the big man. "Quiet…and, yes. Little town two hours north of Toronto."

"Farm?"

"Shht! No, now, enough with the questions."

Properly scolded, Jumbo Joe shut up and walked. Susan held his flashlight while he held the loaded rifle. He hadn't shot much of anything in the last twenty years, but when he was a kid, he could routinely peg off a quarter of a beer bottle at a time with a rusty .22 from about twenty feet. It probably wouldn't impress in any kind of competition, but his buddies thought it was pretty good. He'd only ever shot a rifle this big twice: once while elk hunting with a couple guys from the team the year he'd been traded to Ottawa. The second time had been when he was fifteen at a field party where he was one of four survivors of Larry Ball's moonshine—the rest of the kids had passed out with vomit crusting down their cheeks.

They reached where Susan had witnessed Charli's demise. Her body was gone now, though there were more than enough signs that extreme violence had taken place—more ticks toward believing the woman's story.

"Follow me and keep that light shined on the bush there," Jumbo Joe whispered, stepping slowly toward the scene, avoiding the many blood splotches that marred the white sand.

"Be careful," Susan said.

The flashlight shook minutely in her outstretched hand. Jumbo Joe didn't need anything more steady and was thinking about how much he liked this woman already, in comparison to every other person he'd met since arriving. Having money for one's entire life could take a body far, but it couldn't make a body smart or logical, couldn't make a body be a whole, functioning human being. He decided he'd tell her as much, right after they figured out this misery.

"Come around to the other side of me. I need to put eyes past the coverage," Jumbo Joe said.

Given that he heard no rustling, no activity at all aside from the lapping of the ocean, his worry about the situation was dropping, quickly. He grabbed a branch and pulled.

Susan shined the light, then gasped. There was a great divot in the sand beneath the branch; in that divot was a wash of blood and an iPhone. There was no chance of Charli surviving and not taking her phone or the copious sum of blood she had spilled into the sand.

"Look," Jumbo Joe said, pointing with the long rifle barrel to another gulley a short way into the bush. This one was less obvious as the sand sat atop soil here and didn't allow for as deep a trench. "Something dragged her away."

"What can drag away a whole woman?"

"Was she big?" Jumbo Joe said.

Susan snorted, then covered her mouth. She spoke through her fingers. "No. She was like ninety-five pounds."

"A lot of animals could drag her away, then, wouldn't even need to put in a team effort. But I don't know what kind of animals live on this island. Maybe it was one of those kimono dragons."

"Komodo dragons. A kimono is a Japanese dress, or a sexy robe, or…whatever."

"Ha, yeah." Jumbo Joe looked around the dark forest. It wasn't exactly inviting, but it didn't feel dangerous. "Look, we can go back and, I guess, ring up help from the mainland or we can follow this trail and see where it takes us."

Susan huffed, then breathed deeply through her nose. "We have to look for her."

"I agree. Keep that light steady. Something tells me we're poking around for a gong show," Jumbo Joe said, partly hoping they never found Charli, which might prolong the time he spent with this intriguing, smalltown Canadian woman called Susan. Hell, it might prolong it enough that they really got to know one another.

8

Diana Vega almost didn't take the head cleaner position when the people behind the resort approached her. It didn't matter that they drove nice vehicles, wore swanky suits, or worked in a tall building. She'd watched a documentary about the Fyre Festival and the idea of leaving all those employees high and dry—she didn't care a lick about the rich kids who had to sleep on deflated air mattresses and eat cheese sandwiches—made her sick to her stomach just considering it. The men behind the resort were persistent though, showing her the facilities underway and the employee barracks with a small private beach for their days off. What convinced her was the landing strip and the plane. The landing strip couldn't go anywhere, and the plane was strictly for use in going from Santiago International to Jabali Island. That was a lot of eggs to put in a basket full of holes.

When she got to the island, she sighed in relief. The photos of the buildings matched the truth—too often physical places didn't stack up to what was shown in brochures. Now, in the thick of things, she was all business…mostly business.

Her shift would start at 3:00 AM, and she was so tired after her first workday on the island, that she'd gone to bed before the sun went down. She hadn't even needed an alarm clock, rolling over at 12:28 AM, two minutes before her clock would sing. The automatic coffeemaker was already dripping—those tidbits she heard and smelled.

After doing the usual morning duties, she poured herself a mug of coffee and stepped out to the beach. Distantly, she heard the tunes coming from the dancehall within the hotel, and for once, it was someone she could vibe with—Richie Spice—and she swayed to the beat.

"*She got magic in her touch, in her touch,*" Diana sang under her breath before falling into a necessary hum because she didn't know the rest of the words.

She settled into the sand, her hair still damp from the shower, and sipped her coffee, watching the water lap beneath the moonlight. Even if the guests proved to be awful, she was now glad she'd taken the position.

Behind her, from another cabin, came a great clang, causing Diana to jump. She reached blindly for her coffee mug as she scanned the eight small buildings. Each had three apartments. The only thing she knew for certain was that the sound hadn't come from her cabin. She sipped from her mug, trickling brown fluid onto her work shirt.

"Son of a gun," she whispered, then pushed to her feet.

Another clank rang out. This time it sounded as if it had come from the building next to hers. She stepped toward her unit, swiping at the damp spot. She had five more shirts to match and decided she'd start the day right and change her shirt. She stopped walking to take another mouthful of her quickly cooling coffee.

The loudest clang yet boomed and she stilled. It sounded as if it had come from her building, if not from her unit.

"What the hell!" a voice shouted, a light flicking on a few units to her right.

A shrill scream rattled through the night from her left.

"Help!" another employee said, this voice from the last building in the line.

More screams filled that little section of beach.

Glass shattered from her building, almost certainly from her unit.

She took a step backward.

Something thumped. The screams and shouts were almost constant now. From the hotel came a rattling hip-hop beat, drowning the terror on the employee beach to any potential saviors.

Diana drank deeply from her mug, emptying it. The door to her unit banged, shaking in its frame. She took another step backward. The door banged again. Diana stumbled sideways and in reverse, moving like a drunk until she backed into a palm tree. The door slammed once more.

"Lord, save me," she whispered, then crossed herself.

The door burst open and a huge pig fired through, cracking the doorframe out of shape. Diana dropped her mug, spinning, then gripping the tree. She shimmied, her toes propelling her upward. The pig leapt, nipping at her heels.

"Git!" she shouted, then, "Help! Somebody!"

Further down the beach, doors swung wide and men and women charged out. Some were naked but most were in sleepwear of some fashion. Pigs big as St. Bernards chased each of them. One of the buildings tipped forward after a pig slammed a beam. The roof caved in next with a surprisingly quiet whoomph.

"Somebody!" Diana shouted, trying to make her voice carry to the hotel, wishing for some luck during a break between songs. "Help!"

Carnage ruled the beach. Men and women were being torn apart. Others were being stomped to death. Others yet were being dragged into the forest, alive. One man ran out to the ocean and started to swim to nowhere. No good. Despite its stunted legs, a pig bolted into and through the ocean like a barracuda, catching the man for a feast.

"Somebody!" Diana looked around as several pigs lifted their heads from their prey. "Somebody," she said again, trailing almost into a whisper.

Two more pigs joined the one looking up at her from the trunk of the palm tree. There was no obvious communication between the pigs, then, almost as if they'd practiced their timing, they leaned their mouths to the tree. They began scraping their teeth against the hard, hard wood as they walked in a circle like pagans around a harvest maiden.

"Somebody!" Diana shouted again, understanding now that chunks of wood began to fly as the pigs began to sprint. "Help me!"

It took less than a minute before the tree lost solidity. Diana tried to rock herself toward her cabin, thinking there was hope for her if she could get to a rooftop. The trunk cracked and the tree tipped…toward the ocean. Diana screamed until the heavy landing stole the air from her lungs. Moving on instinct, she grabbed a handful of sand to throw at the first pig she saw.

A pig she didn't see latched onto her hair. It chewed and swallowed and yanked her backward in a single, undeniable jerk. Another pig attacked, from the front this time. Too shocked by the pain at her scalp, she didn't get a chance to throw the sand when the second pig latched onto her arm. The third pig took a leg and the trio pulled in opposite directions like puppies with a Stretch Armstrong doll.

Diana screamed the audible incarnation of agony rather than forming a word. Her scalp began to peel like a wig, the sound was akin to plunging a toilet. Her arm broke beneath the flesh with a dull snap. Her leg popped from its socket creating enough pain to send the woman into oblivion.

Some pigs feasted, some dragged living people away, and at the hotel, the party continued.

9

An ease had settled into both Jumbo Joe and Susan—given where Susan's headspace was when they first set out, this was a notable change. They crunched through the underbrush of the island's forest, following the drag marks and hoofprints. They appeared to be headed toward the volcano, which had last erupted—according to samples taken of the igneous rocks that lie within its mouth—more than 1,000 years ago.

Jumbo Joe was thinking it wouldn't be so bad to check out the volcano…during the day, following the path that led to it rather than bushwacking. The company, he'd spend time with Susan day or night. She hadn't said anything stupid to him yet, which seemed like a record given the people he'd met since retiring. Pretty well everyone wanted him to use his moderate fame to stepstool themselves up to something a little higher. One man came out and asked if Jumbo Joe could put him in touch with Connor McDavid because he was trying to get a sports drink off the ground. Jumbo Joe had laughed at the man and told him sorry, maybe he should try Gretzky or Tiger Woods or LeBron James. Apparently, his moderate fame was meaningless to Susan.

Part of that might be that she didn't recognize him. Suddenly worried she was a nimrod in disguise, he said, "Hey, you ever watch ice hockey?"

"As opposed to field hockey?" Susan said, her light beam playing about a meter before them.

"Ha, yeah. What I mean is, I'm famous." Jumbo Joe closed his eyes—*now who's the nimrod?*

"Famous, huh?"

Jumbo Joe took a low-hanging branch and held it up so that Susan might duck beneath. "What I mean is, do you know who I am, and if you don't, would you act differently if you knew who I was?"

Susan squat-walked to the far side of the tree. "Why?"

Jumbo Joe sighed. "That came out all wrong. Since retiring, I'm meeting only pests trying to monetize my minor celebrity, and I just wondered if you're a pest in hiding."

"Oh. Yes, I know who you are. You're Jumbo Joe Bourque. My dad hates you. You did something to put out Calgary when I was a kid?"

Jumbo Joe laughed, the memory hitting. "Maybe the worst game I ever played. Coach sat me from the first period until the second overtime. I was the only fresh player by then. It was like pond hockey—both the quality of the ice and the pace of play—and I was Johnny on the spot. Straight cheese, roof daddy."

"You scored?"

"That's right. We got swept in the semi-finals, though. I didn't get my Cup ring until last season."

Susan shined the light on Jumbo Joe's face.

"Ever consider people treat you a certain way because you encourage it?"

A flush flashed up Jumbo Joe's collar. "No…I'm sorry. I just…well, shit."

"It's okay."

Susan shined the light's beam to the sandy forest floor, and they continued in silence. Distantly, they heard hooting and the thump of a drumbeat. The party wasn't going to stop until the sun came up or someone cut the power.

Jumbo Joe stepped on strangely soft debris, though when his weight followed through, it crunched beneath his tread. "Hold up a sec," he said.

Susan stopped and shined the light at Jumbo Joe's feet. He had one foot in the air, turned so that he could see beneath the tread. Bird eggs in a flattened nest.

"Thank god. For a second I thought I stepped on an eyeball." He shook his head minutely. "I mean, the way you described—you know, Susan from Ontario, you kind of make me flustered."

"Oh, umm. I—"

From well beyond sight, something was running toward them, snapping branches and crunching through the dried flora on the forest floor. Jumbo Joe lifted the rifle in preparation.

"Point that light. Steady. Hey, announce yourself or I'll light your lamp."

No words responded, but the cracks and snaps continued, drawing closer. Then it appeared some ten feet away, its milky eyes reflecting the flashlight beam. Its snout was coated in blood, which had partially coagulated and was hanging in icicle drips from the flesh. Jumbo Joe didn't wait and opened fire with two rapid shots. Both tore into the beast: one to the chest and one to the face.

"You got it!" Susan shouted.

"Just a pig, I doubt it was responsible for…" Jumbo Joe trailed.

The pig, which had fallen, pushed upright. The flashlight beam passed through its head where its left eye had been. Lumpy grey fluid globbed free from the hole.

"Shoot it again," Susan whispered.

Jumbo Joe chambered another round, then fired. The top of the pig's head all but burst in a chunky mist. The pig dropped sideways. Neither Jumbo Joe nor Susan said anything, moved only enough to breathe.

The pig twitched, pushing to rise again.

"What the hell is with this thing?" Jumbo Joe charged forward. He reared back with his right leg and booted the pig under the chin. The pig's head whiplashed backward, launching what remained of its brain out behind it with a sloshy snap. It fell sideways again, unmoving now. Jumbo Joe loomed over the beast, waiting for motion. None came.

Susan stepped to his side. "It's massive. Is it a warthog?"

Jumbo Joe knelt, turning his head to look at the pig's face—what remained of its face. "No.

It's a regular pig, but huge…and sick."

"How'd a regular pig get so big?" Susan said, awed now.

Jumbo Joe shook his head, rising and moving around to the back of the pig. "Not just a regular pig. This is a juvenile. It's a shoat, not a piglet, but not a boar. Like a teenager."

"How do you…? How is that possible?"

"Bring your light." Jumbo Joe pointed at the pig's back end. "Could be wrong, but I'd say this guy's not mature. See those nuts, or where the nuts should push out like a pair of hand grenades?"

Susan cocked her head and squinted. "That can't be, can it?"

"I guess it can…I'm telling you though, it's a shoat, we always called the shoats and gilts pigs. They're of the same use until it comes time for breeding. But this pig, it was a very sick one, too. Look at all that grey shit…must be rabies or something." Jumbo Joe faced Susan. "I don't mean to be insensitive, but we'd better forget your half-sister for now and head back for reinforcements."

"But you killed it?" Susan said, almost whining.

Jumbo Joe pointed to the sandy forest floor and the many drag marks. "It's not the only pig out here, and I don't care to bump into a full-grown sow or a boar in case they have what this guy had."

Susan swallowed. "Yes, okay," she whispered.

10

With the thumping music behind him, Chester Rudd stepped toward the lobby doors with his cellphone in hand. One of the bellhops had given him a number to text for party items, and for the last two hours, nobody had responded. Chester needed something to take the edge off. Booze was just enhancing his fury—that sonofabitch hockey player had treated him with a level of disrespect nobody had ever dared show him.

He waited another two minutes before stomping to the check-in desk. The silver bell sitting there all but demanded that he tap the button. So, he did, thirty-six times in quick succession. When nobody came, he typed out another text, this one promising that he'd have them all fired—whoever they were.

The doors to outside were wide open, chained that way. The walkway leading up was bathed in bright blue light. Chester paced the lobby, working his way closer to the door and further away from the party. He drew up another text, the most colorful yet, but held off sending it. He'd sent the last one only two minutes ago.

"Ugh, fuck this stupid place!"

An idea struck and Chester stepped to the lobby doors. He reached an arm outside, then hit SEND. Perhaps the messages weren't getting through. He'd once visited a resort in Northern Sweden and couldn't get a single bar, could be the island was shaky too—though his phone showed three bars. He stood, eyes on his phone, arm holding that phone straight over his head.

"Answer me!" he shouted, bringing his arm down.

Straight across from the lobby doors, beyond the red gravel walkway, was thick forest. A fresh, physical need hit him. Chester pocketed his cellphone as he stepped out. He unzipped, pulled himself free, then began to piss into the thick flora.

Footfalls approached from down the path. Chester pushed to force the urine out faster. The crunch of gravel drew nearer. Whoever it was, they sounded heavy.

Chester finished, gave himself a triple shake, then zipped up. He turned and saw the sow walking his way. It was spotty with patches of black fur upon its grey flesh. Its eyes were milky orbs. Its face was gaunt with festering black wounds that leaked chunky grey fluid.

Absently, Chester stumbled to the door, tripping over the top step of four. He got up quickly, attention not leaving the hideous pig for a second, and stepped backward into the lobby. The beast followed, its spine dragging gently against the top of the doorframe.

"You can't come in," Chester said, his voice small as he felt at the moment.

The pig stopped, as if listening.

"Good, now, go away," Chester said, stopping as well.

The pig lowered its hind end, legs vibrating

their tensity.

"Go! Get out of—"

The pig leapt. Chester had no chance to get out of the way as the beast's great abdomen, lined with nipples oozing lumpy grey gunk, leaned on him. His left ankle snapped with a disgustingly twig-like sound at the impact, and he howled. The pig began snorting, sniffing at Chester's scalp.

"Help!"

The pig opened her jaws wide, taking his face and then some, into its mouth. It crunched down as Chester tried to jerk away. The face bones of his skull, as well as all the flesh that covered it, disappeared into the shadows around the pig's gnashing teeth. One of Chester's eyes remained intact, as did his tongue. He began to ululate because he could do no more without a lower jaw. The pig swallowed, then opened its mouth wide once more.

As the great sow chowed down on Chester Rudd, six energetic piglets broke through the lobby door. Two more sows, just as big as the first, followed them inside. The piglets rushed down the hallway toward the ground floor rooms. One of the sows started up the winding stairs. The other sow began head-butting the door that led to the dancehall and bar, after the third strike, keeping in-tune with the Jack Harlow track thumping within.

11

Quinton Hebert—Q to everyone in his life aside from his parents and two aunts—had climbed down off the plane with a bag he'd packed himself but had lost sight of the moment he arrived at the airport, then was reunited with at his seat on the plane. The best way to get a pound of cocaine, two pounds of marijuana, and a cornucopia of pills through the airport was to avoid customs with the aid of maintenance workers and security detail.

Most deliveries he'd done of such a nature, Q flew in Cessna floatplanes—vessels he'd piloted himself. On bigger treks, deliveries across borders, he flew one of the Argentinian military's turboprops. He was all but retired from the bigger deliveries nowadays, but he did enjoy these partial vacation trips. Even when he had to go by commercial airline.

He followed the small crowd in a line. As it was opening night for the resort, the plane would remain grounded for three days, the initial guests filling the sixty rooms until at least then. It was a little after 6:00 PM, and he didn't have his meet-up until 10:00 PM.

At the desk, a young woman with sparkling brown eyes handed over his keycard. He offered her a nod in return then headed on his way. The room was nice, though smallish and the TV had only pay-per-view options and the menu channel. At 7:30 PM, he went to the bar. Rich snobby people and overly cordial waitstaff swarmed busily while innocuous salsa music thrummed gently from the speakers.

Despite the fantastic locale, Q was bored already, and he'd be there three more days.

"Screw it," he said and returned to his room. From the stash, he pulled out the baggy of dried mushroom caps. He guessed that while fresh, they might've featured some really groovy colors, but long dead and desaturated, they were black and grey. He weighed eating loose mushrooms or taking a bite from a chocolate bar and chose to save the chocolate for the deep-pocketed tourists. The caps went down, and he decided to take a walk while he was still all there.

Q got turned around on the walkways through the woods, his tummy tingling gently. After about forty minutes, that tingle moved to his brain and the best solution he could think of to get back, then reach the scheduled meeting place, was to cross through the forest.

The hours began to mount and Q lost sense of himself as a part of a larger world. His notions of duty and the desire for financial gain were gone. He looked at birds and touched plants. He listened to shouts and snorts and growls and tried to mimic them under his breath.

The moon was high overhead when the buyer's remorse set in. Half the time he partook in mushrooms he eventually got down on himself about doing so—the other instances remained a steadily good time.

"Stupid. Stupid," he mumbled as he tromped through the forest, hoping there was a way up the hill directly ahead of him. The sobered part of his mind suggested he was looking at the wrong side of the hill he'd seen when he'd first arrived.

"Hey. Hey," a hissing, feminine voice said from above him.

Q looked up. There was a woman hanging in a tree. He blinked rapidly, then licked his dry lips. "Are you real?" he said.

"Yes," the woman said. "Are there any pigs around?"

"Like police?"

"No. Like animals."

Q looked left, then right. "None that I saw."

"Can you help me down?"

Q scrunched up his face. She didn't need help. "Why don't you float?" he said, almost shouting.

"Shh, there are rabid pigs in this forest."

Q looked around. "Maybe I should come up?"

"No, I'm coming down."

She tipped her legs over the side of the branch, her dress catching at her waist. For a moment, those legs looked like huge wiggly fingers to Q. A foot kicked his shoulder then and the image fleeted, alongside his memory of having it. He took one foot, then the other. She dropped more and he ran his hands along her smooth calves. They were chilly to the touch and made him think of rubber. He pressed his cheek to her foot—it was not soft or smooth, was in fact rough and gritty.

"I'm dropping now."

The woman slipped through Q's grip, but he slowed her enough that her fall hurt little more than her sense of decorum.

"You're real," Q said.

"Are you high?"

"No, I'm Q. Oh, yeah, I am high."

Distantly, a rifle shot flared, then echoed.

"Do you know the way back to the hotel?"

Q laughed. "It's possible I've been wandering around for hours. I was hoping there was a way up that hill. Who are you and what were you doing in a tree?"

"I'm Mary." She turned and looked to the cliff wall and the natural platform high above it—the platform from which she'd leapt to save her life. "I came from up there. A pig made me jump. I'm totally fucking losing it here."

Q pouted his lips Robert De Niroly as he nodded. "You should relax."

"I think we should find another way back." Mary then looked at the duffel bag slung over Q's shoulder. "You don't have any water, do you?"

"No, just drugs."

"Drugs?"

"Uh huh. Help you relax, you know."

Mary paused a moment, then said, "What kind?"

12

"Get back behind me!" Jumbo Joe shouted as two pigs charged through the thick flora at the edge of the beach.

Susan did as directed, all the while managing to keep the light trained on the pigs. Jumbo Joe fired, pulled the bolt, fired, pulled the bolt, fired, and paused a moment. Both pigs were down, grey sludge oozing from their wounds. As expected, both pushed to rise.

"How can they do it?" Susan said.

Jumbo Joe had been wondering the same thing since his first run-in with one of these beasts. He stomped closer, knowing the pigs were at least stunned by rifle rounds and that a swift kick to the chin worked like strawberries and whipped cream on angel food cake. He reared back a foot next to one, struck, then repeated. One pig pitched sideways, its gaping skull mashed into a boot shape from below. The other pig snorted and reenergized, as if Jumbo Joe had given its batteries a shake rather than putting a size 13 boot to its chin.

The pig snapped at him. Jumbo Joe leapt sideways as he chambered a fresh round. Susan let out a whine. The shot echoed; the pig dropped, its brains oozing from its ears, nose, mouth, and from the golf ball-sized hole in its cranium.

Jumbo Joe knelt next to the pig, the rifle across his knees. He waved for Susan to come closer with the light.

"I'm no hog vet, but I don't think a brain's supposed to be moldy. Look at those fuzzy patches. Looks like mold to me."

Susan spoke around an audible grimace. "And the blood, why's it grey?"

Speaking as if to himself rather than to Susan, Jumbo Joe said, "And these eyes should be blind, milky as that."

"You're from a farm, that's why you asked if I was, right?" Susan said, and when Jumbo Joe didn't answer, she squeezed his shoulder. "Hey, you're from a farm, right?"

Jumbo Joe looked over his shoulder. "Yeah."

"Why's the blood grey?"

Jumbo Joe shook his head slowly. "We better get back."

It was Susan's turn to ignore his half of the conversation. "How could they build here and not know about this?"

Brushing his hands on his loose slacks, Jumbo Joe said, "Don't know and we'll be lucky if we never have to find out."

They started walking, side-by-side, the ocean lapping gently to their right. Behind them and to the left was the forest and the handful of walking paths. Ahead of them were the lights of the hotel and the steady thumping of the music.

After a dozen or so steps, Susan said, "I wonder where it took Charli…and where's Summer?"

"Did you call either of them?"

"We called Summer plenty, well, texted her. I

didn't try Charli. I was with her until she died."

"Can you try ringing both?" Jumbo Joe said.

"I don't have Summer's number. Charli was texting her." Susan pulled her phone from her pocket. She found the contact and dialed out. "It's ringing."

Jumbo Joe watched her; the moon shimmered off her eyes like the romantic flicker of candlelight. If he didn't keep his focus on the task, he might form a little crush on this woman.

"Nothing?" he said.

"Nothing." Susan hit END. "So, what's the plan?"

Jumbo Joe yawned. "Guess we go back, inform the hotel's manager, and call the mainland. There's not much can be done. As far as I've seen, this place is equipped to handle a few unruly frat boys and a scuba accident."

"Great," Susan said.

"In fairness to the resort, if you're preparing to deal with freakishly large and probably rabid pigs, you're likely in a padded room somewhere."

A scream filled the night, killing the moot discussion. Barreling down the beach like a hippo from a nature documentary was a sow, her back standing about seven feet off the ground. She had a young man in loose shorts and a tank top by the leg and was dragging him. There was enough blood on her snout and face to support the notion that this young man was not likely her first victim.

"Look at the wheels on her," Jumbo Joe said

as he aimed and fired.

The massive pig pitched sideways, stumbling to her knees, successfully crunching and snapping the young man's leg in the process. Both Jumbo Joe and Susan winced at the sound. The sow climbed upright, latched onto her quarry anew, and continued on her way.

Jumbo Joe tried to chamber a fresh round only to discover he'd emptied the magazine. He worked quickly, Susan recognizing where she needed to shine the light without being asked.

"I think he's gone. That one was twice the size…how can it get so big?"

Jumbo Joe had to breathe deeply to keep his hands steady enough to slide rounds into the magazine. "There's some warthogs in Saskatchewan that get almost that big. Something tells me there's bigger goons yet."

"Why the hell do you say that?"

Jumbo Joe shrugged. "We've seen juveniles, we've seen a mama, now we're waiting on a papa."

"No."

Screams from the hotel filled the night, above the music, above the lapping of the waves, above the endless voice of panic ringing through their brains.

13

Three miles from the resort proper, a pig dragged a woman through the bush and toward the volcano. It charged upon the manmade walking path, climbing the steep grade with ease. Once to the top, the woman's foot came off in the pig's mouth and she tumbled. She was alive, but in shock, unaware of the world around her. The pig bounced on its stubby legs, sprinting after the woman as she rolled off the trail, stopping against the steep tower—one laden with communications radios. Almost playfully, the pig put its head down and leapt.

The tower creaked and swayed at the contact. The pig's skull had cracked and compressed, grey fluid spewing from its ears like gruel from a ladle in a Dickens novel. The pig pushed upright, swaying unsteadily.

Woman secured by her remaining foot, the pig started back up the path. The gravel crunched loosely beneath its swaying steps. Almost back to the top, the pig lost the last of its equilibrium, tumbling and flipping down the steep grade, veering off the path just as the woman had. It nailed the tower again.

The creaking steel was this time accompanied by a violent rattle. One of the big radios dropped, smashing into several dozen pieces upon landing. Three seconds later, the tower pitched and yawed. Gravity dug invisible hooks and the tall conglomeration of steel and concrete crashed into a forest of palm trees and thick shrubbery.

The remaining radios were destroyed. Cellular and internet service were gone in a blink and were not coming back until a crew showed up to fix what had been done—something that was unlikely to ever happen.

The pig rose once more, staggering up the hill, more than half of its skull gone now. Rooting with its crusty snout, the pig pushed the one-footed woman over the lip and down into the volcano. She slid onto the igneous rock bed. The pig attempted to steer her to the hole at the north end of the volcano's mouth, but took a final stumble, its damaged brain slipping free from what remained of its skull.

Minutes passed. Another pig appeared, this one dragging a man. The man had not gone into shock and was fully aware that he'd broken several bones and would be feasted upon as he'd seen happen to others. But he was drunk, and a weekend Buddhist, and accepted that this was where this part of his story would end.

The man was pulled to the edge of the hole, then nosed through. The pig turned back to retrieve the one-footed woman. She went down the hole next. That done, the enlivened pig stepped to the moveless beast and began to eat.

14

"Whoa, look at that," Q said, his words spacey, his eyes wide.

They'd moved slowly, skirting the cliff face, trying to follow it back to somewhere civilized. To calm herself, Mary had asked Q to roll her a joint. To get a little bit higher, Q had joined her in smoking it. If what she said was true, getting a little more stoned couldn't hurt.

That was the thought before the physical proofs began to present themselves.

"I've been wrestling with whether or not I actually saw what I thought, but this…" Mary trailed, hand on the rooted divot in the dirt. The walls of the divot had slashes of red throughout.

"The man you saw die, what was his name?" Q said, looking up at the starry sky.

"Benoit. He was a gigolo and a concierge. The jobs are interconnected here, so it appears."

Q turned to Mary. "He was also a drug dealer, I guess. I was supposed to meet him and give him this." Q lifted the duffle bag some.

"He certainly knew what to do," Mary said. "I only tell you that because I'm positive we're both going to die, and not a lick of what I say will matter."

"Yeah, we're going to die eventually," Q said, again looking to the sky.

"Eventually today, if we run into one of those pigs."

Q grinned. "I'd like to see a huge pig."

Mary didn't argue. Instead, she continued forward. They moved slowly, tripping and slipping often over the rough forest terrain. Now and then they heard a bang, almost certainly a gunshot of some fashion—something that encouraged Mary because it meant people knew. The steady drumbeat had them walking with matching steps as they followed the sounds and the valley's natural exit toward the hotel. They hoped.

"The last time I smoked marijuana it was at a fundraiser afterparty, and the joint belonged to Ben Cohen, from Ben and Jerry's."

"For real?"

"For real."

"That's so cool," Q said. "I did blow with El Chapo."

"Really?"

"Uh huh. In an airport hangar. I'd rather have smoked weed with Ben...did he have any ice cream with him?"

Mary laughed. "At a fundraiser afterparty?"

"I could go for some ice cream now." Q tripped immediately after saying this, landing heavily, but managing to keep from falling on the duffel bag.

"Are you okay?" Mary said after hearing the moan.

"Sure," Q said, over moaning that was drawing closer.

Branches were cracking and fronds were making whip-snap sounds. A grunt now and then sounded, growing louder and louder. A pig, much bigger than the ones she'd seen, tore by them. In the pig's mouth was what appeared to be a bedsheet, and within that bedsheet was a slender figure—the source of the whining.

Mary held her breath as the pig bolted by, while Q whispered, "Oh, wow."

There was nothing to do; there was no way they could help. Whoever was trapped in the net of that bedsheet was done for.

They stood immobile for close to a minute before Q said, "That was a lot of bacon."

Mary motor-boated her lips in frustration. She was tired, terrified, and stoned, and what they'd just witnessed suggested there might not be a safe place on the whole island.

"Think that was a woman it had?" Q said.

"I do. I think she was taken from her bed, which means the hotel might not be safe from them either."

Q was silent for a ten count, then said, "Shitty."

For lack of another option, they carried onward, now following the worn path the pig had used, hoping it would guide them back toward the hotel. Mary had visions of herself on a train bridge, another hog using the trail like a train chugging her way, but would leaping off the path be enough? She thought it probably would be, as long as the pig was distracted by another victim…perhaps this drug dealer she'd found by her side.

15

Ishrat Bedi stepped out of his room with an empty ice bucket. He'd heard a neighbor down the hall slamming a door and was using the ruse of grabbing ice so that he could take note of which room it was, then complain to management come morning. Complaining to management had been engrained in him during childhood and then into his teens; his mother had never missed a chance to demand the world bend to her whims. He looked right, then left, saw nothing, and stepped out of his room. There was an ice machine in an alcove only four doors down.

The carpet beneath Ishrat's feet bulged in places, and great, dirty streaks marred the mingling shades of yellow and brown. He grimaced, lifting a now sodden Versace slipper. A gobby chunk of blood and gristle oozed from the slim rubber tread.

"Two grand a night, and this is what I get?" he whispered, already mentally composing the script to the manager's forthcoming thrashing.

He reached the ice machine, still carrying on with the ruse, and filled his bucket. There was a noise coming from the room directly across from the alcove. Ishrat glanced over a shoulder, only noticing then that the room's door was slightly ajar. He grabbed his bucket, looked left, then right again—there were noises coming from the other side of the building, which he attributed to the party still ongoing. He nudged the door further.

The bucket dropped from his hands. Inside, a massive pig was feeding on a naked man Ishrat had seen on his flight from New Delhi to Santiago. The pig lifted its head, milky eyes seeming to look right through him, then began sniffing.

"Very sorry," Ishrat said and pulled the door closed.

He took one step before the door of the room burst out in a rain of slivered shrapnel. The flung door crunched the ice machine nearly flat. The huge pig had knocked itself down, but quickly shook off the pain and pounced on the jogging Ishrat.

"Help!" was Ishrat Bedi's final word.

—

Julieta Gonzalo couldn't sleep and decided to get a jump on tomorrow's soup of the day, then tackle any prep-work she noticed needing done. She'd have to do it all eventually, it would hardly matter that these weren't the hours she was technically being paid for. Besides, getting room and board made the job's wage feel more like a salary. It wasn't as if she could go anywhere; she couldn't quit, then walk down the street to ask if another restaurant needed a food prepper. They were paying her well and she might as well do her very best.

Bad Bunny was in her headphones. "*Ey, y ya la vi,*" she mumbled along, her voice echoing gently in the empty kitchen as she chopped onions. Tears slipped free and she swiped at her left eye. In that motion, she caught something on her periphery. Something large and dark…but gone. "Going crazy," she said, shaking off the feeling of being watched.

Something else flashed and this time she spun fully, her back to a stainless-steel counter. She held out the knife she'd been using to cut onions. She watched, watched, watched and saw nothing untoward. She turned back to her onions.

A fantastic clatter rang out. Julieta spun on her heels. A huge pig was charging straight for her, sending kitchen utensils out in a shower of shining steel. The pig was to her flank in a blink. Instinct had her slashing sideways, burying the knife to the hilt in the pig's head. It fell onto her, eyes wide, milky, and vacant. Wound in its head oozing grey sludge.

It was the biggest pig she'd ever seen, and by more than a little. At least it was dead.

She pushed as she wriggled and kicked. Almost free, the pig lifted its head, stretching its jaws wide, revealing a mouth full of blackened teeth.

Julieta Gonzalo shrieked, her voice carrying down the pig's throat, until the pig latched onto her face and bit off a chunk of her skull. Now and then, she came to as the creature dragged her through the forest, but not far enough that she comprehended that she was as good as dead or that the pig still wore a kitchen knife through the side of its head. All she saw in her waking moments was blood and the fuzzy underside of a massive pig.

—

DJ Galleta had taken the job on Jabali Island because there were no real options otherwise. Between gambling and coke and a man called Carnicero who'd been looking for him, Galleta had worn out his welcome just about everywhere. The locals knew he was a fallen star, but to visitors, they'd still think him at least a C-list celebrity.

Sure, the job felt a lot like what he'd been doing during his teenage years, DJing weddings, but it was paying and he was a long way from the elements attempting to conjure his ruination. The crowd had thinned, and those remaining were so drunk they wanted only singalong songs.

As Lou Bega's *Mambo No. 5* faded into Spirit of the West's slow opening banger *Home for a Rest*, he stepped away from the DJ table and headed for the bar. A young man, recognizing the song began shouting along, all the while stripping out of his shirt and jacket, then linen pants. Barefoot, the young man did a bastardized Riverdance for the hooting crowd.

"Double whiskey and ginger ale," Galleta said to the bartender.

As the bartender fixed the drink, he said, "First time I've ever seen a whole crowd agree with every song, on one level or another."

Galleta huffed. "This is the least creative playlist I've ever compiled…I'm disappointed in myself."

The bartender tilted his head. "You'd rather they didn't like the music, so, what? So you'll feel outside the norm?"

Galleta took his drink without another word and started back toward his table. The whiskey and ginger sat next to his laptop. He suddenly needed to ruin the fun around him. Almost at random, he opened the MF Doom folder on his external hard drive and dragged over a track.

Ten seconds later, a droning beat and a mumbling, monotoned voice filled the space. The drunken guests all looked at one another, then to the DJ. Galleta raised his glass, eyes on the bartender, then drained the sum, fighting off a cough as he did so. People began to sit. One couple started for the double doors that opened onto the lobby.

Before they got there, the doors opened. In a snap, everybody was up. Six huge pigs rushed inside, headbutting and charging and stomping. The seventh and eighth pigs that entered were twice the size of their huge brethren. The doors to the beach burst inward in a rain of glass shards. Three more of the smaller pigs started picking targets. One target was Galleta.

He didn't run; instead, he dropped down to his knees and crawled beneath the long skirt on the DJ table. Cross-legged, he planned to wait until someone came to correct this issue. He heard screams, bone snaps, blood lapping, and flesh devouring. He also heard people being dragged away, their panicked voices letting him gauge their moving distance.

Minutes began to mount. He covered his ears, the terror ensuing out there was simply too much to comprehend. The table was suddenly flipped—having no effect on the digital playlist, which was currently offering up Ray Parker Jr.'s *Ghostbusters*. DJ Galleta, Banji Allende to his mother, howled until the pig's forehooves slammed into his chest, knocking him flat. The beast shifted its weight and Galleta's ribs folded inward like boney claws, puncturing his lungs, kidney, spleen, and stomach. Blood sprouted in a short-lived geyser from between his lips.

The pig lowered its mouth to his head but didn't bite. It paused there a moment. As if torn, the pig lifted and lowered its stretched mouth several times before grabbing a foot and dragging the corpse away, deferring to the plans of its new nature.

16

Susan had already killed the flashlight and ducked behind a large stone at the edge of the beach where it came into contact with the path to the hotel. Jumbo Joe hurried to duck down behind her. Pigs and sows were racing along the beach, some dragging living victims, some dragging dead victims. The living victims screamed and moaned. The dead ones lost fluids, dampening the drag gullies created by their bodies.

"Where are they taking them?" Susan said.

"Hell if I know," Jumbo Joe said, his eyes pinned to the endlessly energetic beasts. "What I want to know is, what's keeping them moving?"

An idea struck Susan. "Maybe it's happened before." She had her phone in her hands, quieted flashlight in the sand next to her knees. She opened her Firefox app and waited. And waited. "I'm not getting signal," she said, almost like a question.

"Try holding it up," Jumbo Joe whispered.

The current string of pigs had gone by and the beach appeared clear from their vantage, though they couldn't see far into the hotel. Susan held her phone high, watching the space at the top where it typically displayed the connected network.

"Nothing. Maybe I broke the antenna or something. Check yours."

"Mine's in my room. I didn't think I'd need it and I didn't want the temptation; I was supposed to be standing guard in the dance hall like a meat head."

"Oh." Susan let her arm drop to her side. "Wait, if the pigs were coming…they must've gone into the hotel."

"Yeah, I don't think the resort's going to be around long. If anybody's alive in there, they'll be leaving downer reviews on…whatever people leave travel reviews on."

"There's no way they got into rooms, right?"

Jumbo Joe sighed. "Hope not, but I think those pigs might be reclaiming the island."

Susan faced away from the hotel's light and gazed down the darkened beach. "But where are they taking the people?"

Jumbo Joe didn't have an answer, so he stood and stepped gingerly around the five-foot-tall stone they'd hidden behind. There were no pigs in view. He stepped out a little further, now able to see around the corner where the path wound up to the hotel's doors. The front of the building was still standing, so that was something. He let his eyes play along to windows within view. He saw nothing untoward from that distance but also saw no human activity.

"I think it's okay. Think you can keep up if I jog the rest of the way in? I'd rather be somewhere with walls."

Susan stood and brushed sand from her legs. "I can try."

They started off, Jumbo Joe slowing a touch to match Susan's speed. He had nearly a foot of height on her and that translated into stride length, add to that his general physical prowess, if he wanted to, he could be inside in a matter of seconds. Next to a prime athlete, he'd become embarrassingly slow, but next to an everyday woman, he was in elite shape.

It took no more than two minutes, but Susan was gasping by the time they reached the lobby doors. She tried to play it cool; it did not look easy for her.

"Looks like a fuckin' yard sale in there," Jumbo Joe whispered.

"Huh?"

"Uh, I can see a total mess."

From beyond view came snorting and banging and grunting, noises which echoed with the eerie promise of a Halloween sound effects record. Jumbo Joe leaned in close to Susan.

"There's an office behind the check-in desk. It's where I grabbed the rifle. Do you remember the layout of the lobby?"

Susan nodded.

"We'll go in there, use the phone, maybe find some more supplies, and hunker down to wait for reinforcements. Deal?"

Susan cleared her throat, trying to slow her heart rate long enough to say, "Sure thing."

"Okay. Come on. Team effort for the W."

Jumbo Joe ignored Susan's abilities a moment and took nine long strides across the lobby and to the door behind the check-in desk. He glanced back and Susan was shuffle-jogging, hardly lifting her feet. He pushed inside the room and flicked on the light switch. Aside from the gun cabinet, the room featured a carpeted floor, two padded chairs on one side of a big desk and a rolling computer chair on the other. The desk itself was neat and clean, had a day planner, a cup of pens, a keycard on a lanyard, a telephone, and a desktop computer. It looked almost staged.

Susan entered the office and Jumbo Joe closed the door behind her. She moved directly to the computer. It was pin protected. She tried 1-2-3-4, then 0-0-0-0. She huffed when both failed, then tried 4-3-2-1. It worked and the home screen lit. Along the side, where she would've liked to see the little Wi-fi emblem, she saw a slashed circle—no signal.

"Internet's out," Susan said, standing straight.

Jumbo Joe picked up the telephone. No dial tone, no nothing. He chuckled to himself. He needed to select a line or hit nine or something, surely. There were instructions posted on the base of the phone. He followed them and discovered more nothing.

"Phone's out."

"At least we have po—"

"Chsst, shush, don't jinx it," Jumbo Joe said, dead serious. "That's like using the S-word when your tendy's pitching a goose egg."

"Shit?"

Jumbo Joe frowned, scrunching his face. "No. Shutout."

Something crashed not far from the office.

Jumbo Joe hurried to the gun cabinet.

"Ever shoot a rifle?" he said.

"No, but I had a boyfriend who used to make me play *Call of Duty* with him online."

Jumbo Joe's eyebrows went way, way up. "Guess that'll have to do."

17

"I see light," Q said.

They were crouched behind a bush. Pig after pig had charged by, sometimes from behind them, sometimes from in front of them, sometimes heading toward the hotel, sometimes heading toward the volcano. It almost felt like being a kid, watching big rigs fly by, waiting for the right moment to scoot across the highway on a Huffy.

"So do I," Mary said.

"Maybe if we crawl, they won't see us," Q said.

"You're high."

"So are you."

"Let's just run to those cabins, call someone for help, and hide out."

Q huffed. "Fine."

Mary took the lead.

It was quickly obvious things were not okay in the servants' area. Doors were busted open, some lying on the beach, others lying within the cabins. Walls were cracked, two roofs had tipped down into the sand upon crumbled framework. There was blood and signs of violent activity all over the white beach. One tree had been downed.

"Ooh, I'd eat a coconut," Q said, eyeing the felled palm tree.

Mary grabbed him by the elbow, pulling him in tight. "Can't you see we're still in trouble?"

He shrugged.

She yanked him toward the single building that appeared free of damage. Mary tried the first door handle, then the second, then the third. All were locked.

"We need to find some way inside," Mary said, trying one of the windows.

Q nodded, then ran around back of the building. Within seconds, the door of the first unit swung open. Mary was about to ask how he did it when she saw the shared rear wall of the trio of units was gone. This was not the safe haven Mary had been looking for.

Q had opened a refrigerator and discovered a foil takeaway bag full of soggy French fries. He moaned with minor euphoria over the salt and grease. He held the bag out to Mary as he chewed a packed mouthful. She entered the unit and reached a hand into the bag, simply couldn't refuse the offer.

"We should go to the restaurant and order grilled cheese sandwiches," Q said.

Around a gob full of mushed potatoes, Mary said, "Beans on toast."

Q handed off the bag now containing only little fries and overcooked crumbs, then began searching cupboards. In the second, he found a bag of gummy snakes.

"Jackpot!" he shouted.

From beyond the walls of the cabin, a pig snorted in response. Mary stuffed the last of the fries into her mouth as she ran to peek out the door. The biggest one they'd seen yet was about twenty feet away, sniffing at the air. Animal instinct had it using all the tools currently at its disposal. The sow turned its head, its milky eyes dead on Mary at the doorway. The sow snorted once before charging the building.

Mary spun away from the door. “Run!” She pushed Q, his duffel bag bouncing off his hip, the gummy snakes nearly leaping from his shaky grip. “Move!”

Q did. The moment they cleared the ruined rear wall, the sow barreled through the front wall. Running was slow once outside. The deep sand was unconducive to moving quickly, a tail of white grains washing out behind them in waves.

Mary pulled Q into a turn, button-hooking around a tree and heading back toward the buildings. She’d spotted something and thought it might be helpful: the buildings ran on a mix of solar and diesel. The diesel generator at the back of the buildings had been hidden in a small shed. Pigs had shredded the shed, its walls lying flat in the sand. But this was okay, was good in fact. The destruction had revealed the building’s contents, which included a tipped and leaking diesel tank.

“Lend me your lighter!” Mary shouted.

The sow had overshot them thanks to their hooked turn and was clumsily taking a wide U to get back around. Q reached into his pocket and came out with his lighter in hand. Mary snatched it and knelt. She put the lighter to the diesel and…nothing.

"Why isn't it burning?"

Q looked at the fluid, then to Mary, then to the sow, now pointed in the correct direction and coming fast. "How should I know."

Mary lifted the lighter, touched the flame with her free hand—it was a flame all right—and jerked away at the pain. She lowered the lighter again.

The sow was almost on top of them. Q grabbed Mary and yanked her sideways. The sow leapt, crashing into the diesel tank. The fluid burst out, coating the sow's belly and teats. Q and Mary staggered further away. Mary still held the seemingly useless lighter, its steel guards marred by soot and red hot from being held so long.

"Useless twat," Mary said, then pitched the lighter at the sow, striking its ass.

"Hey," Q said.

The sow began a slow, waddling turn. As it did so, it stepped on the lighter, inadvertently rubbing the wheel and stone to create a spark. The lighter fluid barked out a flame. The splashed areas lit, and as the fire burned, the diesel finally caught. A slow wave of flames danced across the sow. There was hope for but a moment. The flames didn't seem to deter the animal.

"Uh oh," Q said.

Mary got to her feet and began yanking at Q. Given that the animal was awful at turns, Mary pulled Q in a sprint ten feet to their right, then jerked 90° to their left a heartbeat before the sow could reach them. They ran into the middle cabin with the destroyed rear wall. There were bits and pieces of human everywhere, the walls Rorschached with red splotches, the carpet soggy with blood. Mary reached the door and fiddled with the deadbolt.

The sow faced them again, still burning and unperturbed about it.

"Damn you!" Mary said, her voice high, panicked, and frustrated.

Q looked around. There was a liter jug of hand sanitizer on the dresser. He grabbed it, running fluid spilling out of its open cap at the pressure. He threw it just as Mary got the door open. The sow snapped at the flying jug, catching it between its jaws, squirting more than half the bottle onto the floor of the room.

Again, Mary pulled Q. He fell over the doorframe and rolled, accidentally toppling Mary in the process.

The hand sanitizer lit, and flames leapt up in a colorful wave, into the sow's mouth. The plastic container leaked steadily and the flames ate it up. Finally, the fire had caught up to the sow and it had to stop running, trying to spit out the jug and all the fluid it had leaked. The flames danced, glowing inside the sow's face like a candle in a jack-o-lantern. The sow snorted deeply and the flames leapt into her sinus. Quickly, the beast's head was engulfed. The sow bucked and jerked, trying to quell the ravenous fire.

Q and Mary watched from the sand, their bodies tangled from Q's defensive maneuvers.

The sow fell sideways, burning, smelling vaguely of pork roast.

"Oh, man, grilled cheese with bacon," Q said, moaning the words. "We'll have to find another lighter, too."

18

The bloodbath was beyond their control.

Now, these pigs moved at undeniable impulses: the first had been bred into them naturally through evolution, which was to feast. The second impulse came much later and much more recently. This was now their prime objective. To secure mammalian life and take it where it *belonged* was an undeniable goal. Why they dragged bodies—living or dead hardly mattered—to the volcano, they had no way of knowing. But they did it, and usually before giving in to their first and genetic impulse to feed—though not always, especially when it came to pigs that were too immature prior to the great change they'd experienced.

The incredible beasts followed scents and sounds, and when possible, sight. Their senses had changed, as had the tools they used to convey those senses into action. Finding people had been simple at first, but after the initial attack, they had to smell for survivors and root through debris for bodies. If people were there, the pigs would find them and deliver them. All of them.

19

Since he knew the layout beyond the lobby and Susan did not, Jumbo Joe took the lead. The hotel was a mess. The carpets and stone flooring had been obliterated in sections, in others, it was merely stained. Almost nowhere did it look as it had that morning or the night prior. Every piece of art that had hung was on the floor. The fireplace and all the heavy accents were toppled or smashed; some were both. The only thing still offering a semblance of normalcy was the music coming from the dance hall. They glanced through the destroyed doors. Within, the bar, all the tables, and flooring were trashed. Blood coated most surfaces and was congealing into dark, tacky splotches.

Jumbo Joe and Susan gave it only a brief glance as they hurried past, but that was enough. Though it appeared the hotel was free of pigs, it didn't feel safe. They skirted the stairs to the upstairs rooms and passed a dozen doors that had been forcefully opened. These weren't guest rooms, so within looked mostly as it should, aside from splintered wood and the occasional streak of blood or goopy grey stuff. Some lights flickered; some were smashed out.

There was a doorway that led out to a pool where fronds, bits of wood, and a single flip-flop sandal floated. Jumbo Joe led them in the opposite direction from the pool and just about anywhere else guests would've been likely to congregate, at least late at night. The dining room was a mess, but by now, the mess was the norm and to be expected. They cut through the large space, each holding a rifle with a flashlight Gorilla-taped to the bottom of its barrel. Jumbo Joe kicked a foot and ankle within a ropey stiletto shoe beneath a table before Susan had to see it. He wondered briefly if, in the modern world, doing so was sexist.

He decided he was probably just too hungry, too tired, and too scared for completely rational thinking. He pushed through what remained of double swinging doors—they'd been bent at the hinges and both had snapped above the handles, leaving gaping holes. Not far from where they stood were strange hissing sounds.

Jumbo Joe lowered to a squat and Susan did the same at his side.

"There's one in the kitchen; hear it?"

Susan nodded slowly, her mouth slack, her eyes red-rimmed, her pallor carrying a hint of green.

Then they heard: "What kind of resort doesn't carry beans in molasses?" The voice was female, British, and decidedly un-pig-like. A scent came to them next, aside from the fryer and refrigeration smells: marijuana.

Still squatting, Jumbo Joe stepped around a corner. To his left was a short hall that ended in a heavy-looking steel door, exit sign glowing above it. To his right were a man and a woman. The woman was filthy, her dress in tatters, her expression sleepy. The man wore a coating of sand, his hair in disarray, his eyes pink and puffy. On the kitchen island was a dirty black duffle bag, and next to it was a tea saucer working like an ashtray for a lit joint.

Susan followed next to Jumbo Joe, squat-walking. Once she saw the pair busily fixing a meal, she stood and said, "Hello?"

20

Both Mary and Q leapt when they heard the unexpected voice. Q began laughing and Mary began crying. In the last twenty minutes or so, the subject of whether or not anyone had survived had come and gone, come again and left again. The consensus between them had been that it was unlikely that the pigs had gotten *everybody*.

Now, they were making grilled cheese sandwiches with onion rings…if the damned deep fryer would ever heat up. They'd lit another joint as they waited, Mary suggesting she might as well, given that the remainder of her life could be easily calculated down to minutes or hours. Probably.

"Who are you?" Mary said.

"I'm Joe Bourque and she's Susan," Jumbo Joe said.

"Marshall, Susan Marshall." Susan crossed the room with her free hand out, the rifle in the other, hanging at her side.

Mary accepted the offered hand. "Where have you been?"

"Where have *you* been?" Jumbo Joe said. He stepped closer but did not offer his hand.

Mary spoke quickly and quietly while Q continued to cook. Once Mary was finished, Susan gave a rundown of all they'd been through.

"You killed one with fire?" Susan said.

"It only died once the fire crawled into its head. It was like it didn't care until then. The fire was almost useless," Q said, turning from the fryer with the huge plate of onion rings. "Enough for everyone." He and Mary had already eaten their sandwiches.

"So, what should we do?" Mary said. "I was thinking the pantry seems safe, and eventually someone has to come."

Jumbo Joe stood from the stool he'd pulled up next to the kitchen island. He stuffed a final onion ring into his mouth as he walked.

"The phones and internet are out," Susan said.

"That's quite a ring," Q said, sleepy-eyed, voice dopey as cough syrup.

Jumbo Joe ignored this, trying to listen beyond the steel door with the exit sign above.

"It's a championship ring. For pro hockey," Susan said to Q, then turned back to Mary. "Is the pantry big?"

Mary stood, pointing to a heavy white door with a galvanized steel handle.

"He looks like a hockey player. I lived in Canada for a while when I was a kid. My dad moved us around, like everywhere, all over the world. I lived in a suburb outside Vancouver for most of a school year—sixth grade." Q took a deep drag from a fresh joint, then added, speaking with his breath held, "People were nuts over hockey."

Jumbo Joe reached the door. He pushed the paddle, opening the door just a crack. He peeked out, not a foot away was a massive beast. Jumbo Joe saw only a drippy black mouth with a massive white tusk before he pulled the door closed. That mouth had been eye-level. About six feet high. Walking backward, he rejoined the group.

"It won't be comfy if we have to stay awhile," Mary said, defending her suggestion that they stay in the pantry. "But I was thinking, the pigs' eyes look blind, so if they mostly rely on their noses, it might be better to hide in a stinky place."

"We need to get higher. We can't stay here. Fill your pockets with food and water, then we need to go," Jumbo Joe said, still looking at the steel door.

"Why you looking at the door?" Q said, then held out the joint. "Want a hit?"

Susan and Mary turned from the pantry doorway.

Jumbo Joe swallowed, still refusing to take his eyes off the door. "There's a boar. A full-grown boar, full-grown by Jabali Island standards. Bigger than the biggest goon I ever dropped 'em with, and then some. Must stand around nine feet. Grab food and water, then we need to find our way to the roof. No more talking, got it?"

Susan and Mary nodded.

Q pulled the package of gummy snakes from his pocket and said, "Su-nakes! Yeah, boy!"

21

"You silly sonofabitch," Jumbo Joe said, the door thumping behind him in emphasis. A following thump had a tusk puncturing the steel. "Quick, grab what we'll need!"

Q opened his duffel bag. There was room, though not a great deal of it. There was a stack of cases of Fiji water around the corner of the pantry. Sixteen bottles fit neatly. Q frowned, then took half of them out to get to the cocaine. He took the two packs out and stuffed them into his back pockets. All twenty-four bottles fit then, and he lowered himself beneath the strap, groaning when he stood as the strap dug into his neck with the new weight in the duffel bag.

As Q worked, Mary and Susan busied themselves at filling a garbage bag with crackers, chips, and a wheel of cheese. For the most part, the food at the resort was from scratch, leaving them with less-than-ideal options. Once the bag was mostly filled, Mary slung it over her shoulder like she was Santa Claus of Christmas Eve, about to bring high-fiber options to kids around the globe.

Jumbo Joe let them work. He stood sentinel at the T-corner that split between the hallway to the dining area and to the hallway where a boar was currently testing a door that was warping further out of shape every handful of seconds. There'd be no shooting until he knew it was absolutely worthwhile to do so. No sense filling an inanimate door with rounds from a limited supply.

He kept an eye and an ear to the dining room. The way the pigs had come and gone, dragging away victims, suggested they were driven to eradicating human life on the island—not that he thought their minds worked all that well, given how moldy and goopy they proved to be.

The door outside bent far enough that the boar could look through now. Once he spotted the survivors, he snorted, then made a high growling sound, and finally backed away.

"Time to boot scoot and boogie!" Jumbo Joe said.

Mary and Susan were quickly behind Jumbo Joe, who led them down the hall toward the dining room. Q was straggling behind, trying to get comfortable with the strap rubbing his neck. He had to stop, leaning as he fiddled with the resting location of the heavy bag. The door burst open and a chunk of frame spun through the room, a sharp edge nicking Q's neck—had he been standing straight, the wood would've nailed him in the nose and mouth.

"Holy smokes," he whispered.

"Come on!" Susan shouted over her shoulder.

Q did his best, catching up to the others only because they'd slowed down.

The dining room was a mess, though no more alive than it had been on their first pass on the way to the kitchen. They were no less leery that something might appear. It felt as if the pigs could be anywhere.

"Stick together," Jumbo Joe said, still in the lead. "A strong defense is the best offense."

They stuck together, Susan changing spots with Q so that she could mind the rear. They passed through the dining room and were back in the hall featuring the various closets and workspaces. Still, no pigs.

Their pace slowed in the lobby. Danger could come from most angles, and the main entrance seemed like the only place the boar might get through—Jumbo Joe felt okay about the pigs, felt uneasy about the sows, and was terrified of that boar…if there indeed was only one.

"Mary, hand your goodies to the dumbass and run on in there and grab yourself some firepower," Jumbo Joe said.

Mary handed her bag to Q.

"Hey, wait," Q said, only then realizing that he was the dumbass.

"Zip it, eh?" Jumbo Joe said, not looking at Q.

Mary appeared with two handguns and a jingle to her step from the canvas bag of bullets she'd grabbed. "There were no more that matched the big one, I think…right?"

"Likely," Jumbo Joe said.

"And I'm the dumbass?" Q said, sulking.

"I swear to the Lord above, I will put my mitts so deep into your noggin you'll think you sprouted arms from your face." Jumbo Joe gestured with his rifle behind them, to the stairs. "We need to find a way to higher ground."

Susan led the charge this time, Mary at her side. Q was struggling with the bags, but Jumbo Joe waited for him.

"We had a lazy mule on the farm once. Dad got it on a trade for a lawnmower. Damned thing would hardly walk parade speed." Jumbo Joe sneered at Q. "I'd rather have that mule than your pylon ass—"

From the lobby came a tattoo of hooves on the stone floor. Grunts and snorts followed. All but Jumbo Joe picked up the pace. He turned and readied to face off.

22

"There! Grab a chair from a room!" Susan said, pointing to the attic access in the hallway ceiling.

Jumbo Joe remained two steps from the bottom of the stairs, taking aim at a pig clopping across the stone floor. He took a deep breath, and waited, waited, waited, fired. The pig jerked back, stumbling sideways into a wall that did not fare well beneath the immense weight. A light fixture went out, then another and another. The lobby fell into near-total darkness.

The shot pig blinked, its milky eyes shining beneath the light coming from the staircase. Distantly, near the doors by the sound of it, more pigs grunted and snorted and clopped hooves against the stone floor.

"All I need is a little daylight," Jumbo Joe whispered, aiming between the pig's eyes, "and I'll snipe a bb, pop your scalp to the rafters."

He fired, the pig bucked, then flopped, a grey puddle expanding beneath it.

The pigs across the lobby came running and Jumbo Joe retreated. Q was all that remained on the floor, his duffle bag and the garbage bag of food were already topside. He climbed onto the chair, Susan and Mary taking hold of his arms. He disappeared in a blink.

Jumbo Joe gave a glance back before he climbed onto the chair himself, tossed his rifle up, then reached for the edges of the frame. A pig came barreling at him, blowing the chair to smithereens and sending Jumbo Joe cartwheeling behind it.

Q ducked his upper half out of the attic. “That’s not good,” he said.

Jumbo Joe was already running back toward the attic as the clumsy pig made a four-point turn in one of the doorways.

“Is there a ladder up there?” Jumbo Joe said.

“Get out of the way,” Susan said from beyond view.

Q climbed over the hole, a baggy of cocaine falling from his back pocket. The baggy burst onto Jumbo Joe’s face. He blinked and shook his head in rapid strokes, sending out cloudy white puffs when he exhaled.

The pig had turned around and was running. From the stairs, came another pig. Susan was working at lowering a loop of thick wire she’d pulled off the ceiling in a rain of staples.

Jumbo Joe did not see the wire. His mind was too busy doing creative, life-saving math. He reared back, his fist cocked behind his hip, then punched a hole about three feet high in the wall. Moving faster than he had in more than a decade, Jumbo Joe leapt, using the hole as a toehold, and sprung himself into the attic high enough that he landed heavily on a rib.

As he scrambled the rest of the way, thc two charging pigs had a head-on collision below. The crack was incredible, sending a vibration up through the floor of the attic. One pig’s skull flattened almost completely, grey goop flying from its ears and snout like projectile vomit from a kid taking their first ferry ride.

Jumbo Joe rolled onto his side in the attic and looked up at the others. He began nodding, grinning, and said, “Let’s go, boys. We got ‘em now!” His eyes were like lanterns in the dim space.

“I dropped half my coke,” Q said, looking down at the powdery mess mingling with the grey goop from the dead pig. He then looked at Jumbo Joe’s white, white face. The math was slow but came together. “How you feeling?”

Jumbo Joe pushed to his knees—the attic was nearly high enough for him to stand—and said, “If I felt any better, I’d have to pull my dick out.”

From several feet away, along a wall, Susan shined the rifle-flashlight at a wooden access panel next to a collection of wires. “I think I found a way we might get to the roof.”

The others crawled, careful to keep to the joists and off the shiny insulation, over to Susan. Jumbo Joe again took the lead. He tore the panel off, then stuck his head and shoulders out the hole—his biceps scraping on both sides.

“This’ll do,” he said before snatching up his rifle to toss it to the roof. He followed it, and only a few seconds later he dangled in front of the hole, his arms stretched. “Who’s first?”

23

The juvenile pigs were gathered below, as were the sows. The boar was nowhere to be seen. Jumbo Joe stood over Susan and Mary, explaining how to match the sight at the end of the barrel with the sight just past the ejection port.

"See that pig, the one with the already smashed head?" Jumbo Joe said, the words tumbling out of him in a rush. "Laser that baby between the eyes."

Q sat behind them drinking water and eating crackers, a joint burning in the tarred gravel next to him—he'd found a fresh lighter in the kitchen. The remaining baggy of coke had been reunited with the other drugs in the duffel bag. The water bottles had been displaced and set next to the garbage bag of food.

Susan aimed, took a breath, and fired. The rifle bucked some, but the pig toppled. Susan leapt to her feet in excitement.

Jumbo Joe grabbed her around the hip in a half-hug. "Susan, Shooter, Mmm—McLean?"

Susan, smiling up at him, said, "Marshall."

"Susan, Shooter, Marshall."

"Might I have a try?" Mary said. She still wore her ruined dress and soggy slip-ons but hadn't complained an iota.

Susan freed herself and knelt to hand off the rifle with the kind of respect deserving of a deadly tool. Mary took the rifle in her thin, bourgey grip. The pig Susan had shot did not rise, so Mary needed another target.

"Which one?" Mary said.

Jumbo Joe popped down next to her, landing on his elbows and hips. "Alrighty, alrighty, alrighty, let's pick you a winner."

"Curious, have you done cocaine before?" Mary said.

"Nope, but one time I played with a Russian in Washington who did a line between periods. Fucking maniac was thrown out of the faceoff circle three out of five times. Hell of a hockey player, though."

"Interesting," Mary said, aiming the rifle from pig to pig to sow to pig until she spotted one that had taken enough damage that a medium distance rifle shot might do some good. "How about that one?"

"Oh, yeah, good pick," Jumbo Joe said, bouncing a little to the thump still coming from the DJ's system.

Mary inhaled deeply, aimed, and shot. The pig went down for a three-count before rolling to stand. Mary exhaled, the sound dripping with disappointment.

"You nailed it. These damn things are like zombies, but made of stronger stuff, and they're pigs," Jumbo Joe said. "Zombie pig…sounds like a fucking ECHL mascot."

"Hey, hockey man, want to even out?" Q said, holding a freshly rolled and lit joint. "You're a bit ADD."

"What? I feel great." To prove this, Jumbo Joe

rolled to his back, then leapt to his feet without using his hands.

Mary set the rifle down and crawled to reach Q's outstretched hand. "Something I hadn't known before: pot makes time move faster."

Susan pouted her bottom lip. "Really, I thought it did the opposite."

Mary took a drag, then held the joint out to Susan. Susan took it and puffed, coughed, and tried again.

"That stuff makes me all tingly and scratchy, is that normal?" Jumbo Joe said, itching at his arms and back in a self-hug. "And my hands." He wiggled his fingers, pausing to slip off his diamond-studded championship ring. "Geez Louise, like someone put fleas in my blood."

"That'll get you until you re-up. The hard stuff can be a bit tricky for newbs," Q said.

Below, the pigs and sows started whining and braying like angry goats. Jumbo Joe leaned over the edge to see if there was something he was missing, all the while itching beneath the ring finger of his right hand.

"What has them riled?" Mary said.

"I don't—"

A fantastic honking bray rang out, startling Jumbo Joe. The ring flew from his grip. A high-pitched squeal left him as he reached, swatting for the object far out of his reach as it seemed to float in slow-motion.

Susan saw the ring bounce and swatted out a hand, catching it. "Got it," she said.

Wide-eyed, almost euphoric, Jumbo Joe said, "I think I love you."

Susan bounced the ring, feeling the weight, then slipped it onto her right thumb. "It's so big."

"That's what she said," Mary said, then covered her mouth, giggling thanks to the marijuana.

Jumbo Joe took a step toward Susan, his hand before him, palm up. Another honking bray rang out a moment before a loud crash shook the building. All but Q shot their arms to their sides for balance. Another crash sounded. The rear corner only ten yards from where Susan stood tumbled toward the ground. A moment later, the boar appeared, snorting and huffing, coated in dust. The pigs and sows began attacking the structure. The broken down corner deteriorated further and Susan did nine consecutive back rolls until stopping six feet from the sand of the hotel's backyard.

"Help!" she shouted.

Jumbo Joe started toward her, emptyhanded. The boar did too. Jumbo Joe dove and slid, his arms outstretched. Susan reached for him, but the boar was faster.

24

Q and Mary ran, ascending to the second section of the roof—an area unperturbed by the destruction done by the boar, followed by the pigs and sows. Q, of course, grabbed his duffle bag. Mary had Susan's rifle.

Jumbo Joe had gotten to the edge and had to struggle his way back as snapping mouths jerked ever closer to taking bits of him. He rushed up the angle, looking over his shoulder the entire way. He scooped up his rifle, then the handgun and the bag of ammunition. He had two boxes of rifle rounds still in his pocket, and enough rounds to fill the handgun two additional times—Mary had loaded it upon reaching the roof.

"Damnit, damnit, damnit!" Jumbo Joe wrenched at his hair, watching the boar peel away. "Damnit!"

"Get up here!" Mary shouted, firing rounds at the beasts stepping onto the lowered corner of the roof. The angle did little to deter them. "Come on!"

Jumbo Joe let off sixteen rapid rounds with the handgun, shooting almost blindly as he pushed further up the roof. Beneath him, the building creaked and groaned. The corner nearest the one that had already crumbled tipped as well, sending out a great puff of dust and a raucous clatter of destruction. Jumbo Joe slipped when the roof beneath him shifted. He began to slide on the tarred steel, firing once before hearing only clicks from the handgun. He brought up the rifle just as his feet came into contact with a sow's snapping mouth. His boots matched her jaw's movements as he fired, pulled the bolt, fired, pulled the bolt, fired. The third shot blew a baseball-sized hole in the middle of the sow's forehead. Grey gunk puddled out in chunky waves as the beast tipped sideways.

Jumbo Joe dug in and kicked, rising just ahead of a pig hot behind him. Jingling with ammunition and coming down from the best bits of the cocaine high, he leapt for the edge of the next portion of the rooftop. Mary and Q grabbed for him as the other section of roof, now busy with massive beasts—thankfully, all had trouble with the swaying beneath their hooves—began to topple.

At the very edge, Jumbo Joe's boots clung where the blocky heels gave space for the rest of the tread, like a car teetering over a mountainside. He nearly tipped backward, but Q and Mary yanked him forward and he fell, sprawling onto the next portion of roof.

He jerked around, trying to work the clip free from the handgun. Distantly, the boar raced along the beach, barely visible above the trees. Susan appeared to be clinging to the beast's tusk.

"Hey, you know what we should do?" Q said, pointing about a mile away, beyond much sand and some forest to the long stretch of asphalt that was the runway. "We should take the plane right back to Santiago. Leave these pigs behind."

Mary faced him, her mouth and eyes like gaping wounds.

"Yeah, and who'd fly the plane?" Jumbo Joe said, pacing.

"Me."

Jumbo Joe stopped and looked at Q.

"What?" Q said when Jumbo Joe frowned, tilting his head as if considering a two-headed donkey. "I never flew something that big, but close."

Mary's expression lit up with hope.

"We ain't going anywhere until me and that there boar drop the mitts," Jumbo Joe said, gazing longingly toward the forest and volcano. "You said they were headed up that way, right?"

"You're going to save her?" Mary said.

Jumbo Joe said nothing to this and began looking over the unexplored edges of the roof. There had to be something, anything that could take him past the conglomeration of beasts hanging around the hotel. They were animals and he was a person; this fact had to be worth something in a combat situation.

25

"You're going after her?" Mary said—what she didn't say was, *if you're going after her, who will protect us, who will protect me?*

Jumbo Joe didn't respond directly. "We need a trick play, a diversion."

"Something brought the pigs out tonight, and not before," Q said, his words spacey, his fleeting focus mostly on the night sky. "Is Mercury in retrograde or something?"

Jumbo Joe leaned over an edge to look down at the milling pigs and sows. The boar hadn't returned.

"Wait…on the brochure…so, they didn't build the resort here, they only tacked it together after running the hydro. They brought it in by boat and only had to add the marble for the floors and fireplaces. Virtually everything was together," Mary said, the words tumbling from her excitedly.

"And?"

"So, maybe the pigs didn't hear the workers, but they heard the guests—the guests and the music! It wasn't even when we first got here, it was later, right? Maybe when the music started, or sometime thereafter." Mary stepped over to Q and snatched the burning joint from his fingers. She took a puff, then exhaled, and spoke around the smoke in a held-breath-pitch. "Maybe we quit the music?"

"What if they're like werewolves and only

come out beneath a full moon," Q said.

"No. No. Nope. Not a full moon," Jumbo Joe said absently. "They must've made some noise putting this place together, can't be the music and can't be the moon."

Mary handed the joint back to Q. "What if it's a mix? The sound starts, but that's not enough. The sun fully goes down, then Bob's your uncle."

"So, we wait until morning?" Q said. "Wish we hadn't lost all the snacks."

Jumbo Joe had stepped to the edge of the roof, two sections from where the others sat, and looked down. The gulley between the building and the forest was only ten or so feet. There was a small shed there and two two-seater ATVs. He tapped his chin in thought. He doubted they could wait until morning; sooner or later, the pigs would take down the rest of the hotel to get at them.

Mary and Q sat silently, sharing the only water bottle to survive the crash of the first part of the hotel. Below, it sounded as if the animals were becoming restless; there was no chance they could stay put. This was a time for action.

Jumbo Joe stepped to the edge of the roof that aligned with the kitchen. He looked out, toward the staff area of the property. Surrounded by trees, though in a clearing, was a dark propane tank—likely that dark paint was a similar green to the palm fronds or a brown similar to the palm trunks, but at night it looked black. Obviously, the tank was hiding without really hiding as it needed to be close to the building, and yet, for peace of mind, it couldn't be *too close*.

Two plans he'd been ping-ponging around his high-wired mind were beginning to mingle. He needed to get to the volcano—he'd consider the return trip once that hurdle had been jumped. Q and Mary had to get to the plane. Both needed a grand distraction to keep the beasts occupied.

"Hey, shoot a pig over that way," Jumbo Joe said, pointing toward the main beach, "I need to check something. You, dumbass, come down here and shout if a pig comes for me."

Q laughed. "You have me confused and it's hilarious." He stood and followed Jumbo Joe.

Mary took aim from the furthest possible place on the roof and fired. The pigs seemed to focus on the noise, and none were in the slim space between the back of the hotel and the forest, none even glanced in that direction. Jumbo Joe stepped lightly onto the roof of the shed, finding his limbs feeling heavy, exhausted, making it tough to move quietly. He leapt to the grass and paused a moment to scan the darkness around him for eyeshine. When there was none, he stepped to the matching two-seater ATVs.

"Hmm," he said as he leaned beneath a thick roll bar that bordered the cab.

The keys were there, but the vehicles appeared to be electric, and he had little faith in the power of a small electric engine next to a gas-powered unit of similar size. Still, with the keys in both, they should be able to use them. Jumbo Joe hit the ignition button of the first ATV. The lights lit, but there were no other sounds. Maybe electric would prove beneficial.

He said, "Hmm," once again before killing the engine and sliding into the second ATV.

It started as well. After that, he went around to be certain they were free of obstruction—he unplugged both, the only obstruction he noted. He pulled the first ATV in tight to the little shed and climbed back onto the roof.

"Those look tight, man," Q said, leaning over the edge of the roof.

Jumbo Joe didn't reply, instead stepping up behind Mary, just as she potted a third shot into a previously battered sow. The beast tipped, but within seconds was up once more.

Another sow began headbutting a wall. Mary pushed to her feet and nearly threw the rifle, startled by Jumbo Joe's nearness after being so intently focused. The pigs and sows were growing louder and more active below.

"Here's the plan. I'm going to peg off the fitting at the front of the propane tank. If it doesn't light right away, I'll keep shooting until there's a big enough spark. Once she's burning, you two take one of those electric ATVs to the plane and I take the other to the volcano. You get the plane ready for takeoff and wait for me, see if you can't get someone on the radio." Jumbo Joe scowled at Q. "You better not have been bullshitting when you said you could fly a plane."

Q snorted a laugh. "Yeah, or what? You'll beat

me up?"

"No," Jumbo Joe said. "You'll die first, though. If we're all going to die, you'll die first."

Q's grin slipped.

"Now, give me the baggy of coke," Jumbo Joe said.

Q sneered. "*He's strong to the finish because he snorts up his spinach, he's douche bag the haw-key man.*" He then pulled the huge baggy of cocaine from his duffel and handed it over.

Jumbo Joe sniffed, his nose suddenly runny and a little itchy and a lot ready for more blow.

26

Jumbo Joe lay on his tummy, breathing deeply in an attempt to slow his heart and steady his hands as he eyed the steel coupler at the front of the propane tank some fifty or sixty feet away. For a moment, his mind flew back to the farm and the beer bottle targets he'd set up in front of round straw bales. He and his buddies had set it up to be a competition, but Jumbo Joe—known as Legs Bourque back then—had no real test to overcome, had nothing more than bragging rights on the line. Now, everything was on the line.

He fired, pinging off the tank about an inch from his target. He chambered a fresh round, popping the spent casing free. He aimed, correcting his previous mistake, and fired again. Instantly, the tank began hissing.

The pigs and sows had begun to gather beneath where Jumbo Joe lay, his forearms and rifle overhanging the building. Two pigs began headbutting the wall beneath him, sending a shimmy up to the roof; a shimmy which grew a little more pronounced with each strike, suggesting this section of the hotel didn't have long to stand.

Jumbo Joe was about to fire again when he thought better of it. There were many more shots with a handgun at their disposal, and they were far less impactful when it came to the beasts of Jabali Island. He aimed the handgun from a standing position. He fired once, twice, and the third time was the charm as the shot nailed a galvanized coupler, sending free a shower of sparks that lit oxygen and propane fumes in a roiling balloon of light.

"Look at that," Mary said, awe in her tone.

After the initial flare, the propane tank began acting like a flamethrower. The blue fire reaching at least ten feet in a cone of destructive light. The pigs and sows hurried over. Trees began to burn, as did the felled debris littering the forest floor.

"Better move. Possible she'll blow," Jumbo Joe said.

Mary and Q were already at the edge and started down. Once they were beyond view, Jumbo Joe took the coke baggy and put his nose in the little tear he'd made. He snuffed back a helping that painted his nose and upper lip white with dust. The baggy went into a back pocket as he rushed to the edge of the hotel, feeling a lot like Superman.

Mary manned the second rifle while Q drove the nearly silent ATV. They were already on their way by the time Jumbo Joe climbed off the utility shed. He hopped into the second ATV and took a wide route through the trees. Within a minute, he found himself at the destroyed employee area. The white sand was streaked with blood and the buildings had all toppled. Thankfully, there was nary a pig in sight.

As suspected, the ATV didn't have the power of a gasoline engine, but it was better than he'd assumed. He kept up a steady clip of about 30

MPH, bouncing and rattling around in his seat. He used the lights in the thick forest, even when he stumbled upon a relatively smooth trail cut into the earth. Stomped into the packed soil were bits of cloth and chunks of human flesh which were made visible by streaks of blood preceding and following. He rolled by hats, wallets, cellphones, the bric-a-brac resort guests wouldn't need in the afterlife. This had to be the right path.

The volcano seemed a long way off, but he was getting there. Not for a moment did he consider survival over the rescue mission. That was not how Jumbo Joe Bourque operated. You didn't win a game by planning the afterparty, you won by executing the work it took to get to the afterparty.

By the time he reached the bottom of the slope that would eventually ascend to the volcano, he was starting to feel okay about the forest. His attention bounced as his eyes scanned, the input coming to him and being considered at lightning speed thanks to the cocaine. The stuff was like magic powder; it wasn't a wonder why so many became addicted to it. He felt that if the ATV broke down, he'd likely be able to leap a few dozen strides and arrive at his destination almost as quickly.

The good feeling crashed the same moment he heard a large tree crack and fall. It happened to his left and he watched the woods behind him, his head jerking back and forth on a snapping swivel to be sure he didn't go off-trail or simply crash.

Seconds mounted and Jumbo Joe saw nothing untoward. He reached a clearing at the base of the volcano. Here he spotted the demolished communication tower and the dead pig that had felled it. He could focus on this only a few moments before another tree crashed, this time directly behind him.

There was the boar, keeping pace, following Jumbo Joe up to the volcano.

27

Mary tried to hold the rifle steady as she scanned the woods for life. She'd taken one, perhaps two, too many hits off the joints for this kind of operation. The vibration from the rough terrain and her bouncing in her seat had her fighting off fits of the giggles. How a situation could be equal parts deadly serious and outrageously funny seemed impossible. That impossibility had her laughing harder, which made scanning the world for ravenous predators wildly difficult.

Q seemed fine, adjusted to existing with weed in his system. The ATV had a steering wheel rather than handlebars. The accelerator pedal, as well as the brakes, were controlled at his feet rather than with thumb and finger, which was the norm for ATVs.

Now and then, Mary spotted a bird, otherwise the forest was lifeless. The route to the airplane wasn't exactly mapped out, and Q—without discussing it with Mary—was taking an untrodden path, cutting and weaving between trees, rocks, and holes rooted into the soil.

The grey of the fresh tarmac came into view and Mary hooted, covered her mouth, then proceeded to laugh until gasping. Q looked at her and began laughing himself. Neither saw the trouble ahead. The front left wheel of the ATV caught a divot and launched them into a roll. Q bounced onto Mary a heartbeat before being fired as if from a cannon, out the front of the vehicle. Mary had on her seatbelt—though it was loose from the last passenger—and managed to stay within the roll cage until the ATV quit twisting and pounding against the edge of the runway. The duffel bag was gone, and the rifle was gone.

The engine was still sending power to the rolling wheels and the headlights remained lit, despite that it leaned against a tree, mostly on its roof.

Mary unbuckled, dropping heavily. “Bollocks,” she whispered. Crawling, she got herself free.

Q was about fifteen feet away from the ATV’s final resting place, moaning and rolling on his back like a turtle on its shell. Mary jogged to his side, scanning his body for obvious damage.

“You okay?” she said.

Q opened his eyes, shifted to his side, then vomited the water he’d drank and the crackers he’d eaten. “Am now. Guess we’d better blow, huh?” he said.

“Yeah. I lost the rifle…and your drugs.”

Q unbuttoned, then reached into his breast pocket, and upon finding what he sought, patted it. “We’ll be okay.”

“Only if we can get on that plane,” Mary said, helping Q to his feet.

They were not far from the runway and hobbled slightly faster than walking over to the rolling stairs. The stairs had an electric motor and moved silently over to the plane.

"How does it open?" Mary said.

Rather than explain, Q climbed the steps, pulled out the swinging handle, gave it a spin, and heaved. The door opened a crack. Q bent to get a grip on an inner handle. The door then swung easily.

Q smiled at Mary. The expression fell quickly as he gazed back the way they'd come. The forest nearest the hotel was alight. It wouldn't be long until the entire island—aside from the runway and the beaches—was a big splotch of soot.

"Smells like a pig roast," Q said.

"I hope they all burn," Mary said, unaware that the crashing of the ATV would send one of the sows chasing their way when the rest of the sows and pigs burned—somewhat—alive.

28

The angle of the path up the side of the volcano was steep enough that twice Jumbo Joe had to rock back and forth to put weight on different spinning tires. Luckily, the boar slowed on the stark grade as well.

The ATV hit the rocky lip at the edge and caught air, almost as if launched onto the black floor within the volcano. So smooth was the hardened lava that when Jumbo Joe attempted to stop, the vehicle began to spin. He clenched his teeth and gripped a roll bar and the rifle until he came to a stop some forty feet from where he'd entered.

The boar climbed topside and paused a moment. It suddenly felt as if he was a gladiator in Caesar's arena. He reached into his back pocket. The baggy had ripped and he felt the powder on his fingers. He rammed the index and middle up his nose, then popped them back into his pocket for a second helping, not unlike a kid with a Fun Dip packet.

The boar started running. Jumbo Joe put the rifle against the steering wheel. That wheel was pre-emptively turned as far to the left as it would go, and his foot hovered above the accelerator pedal.

Jumbo Joe sang, "*Come, come, come, come, come, come my baby, you're my butterfly—*" only stopping to fire, pull the bolt, fire, pull the bolt, then slam his foot on the accelerator.

The boar lowered its head and came up swinging with its tusks, missing the ATV by inches. It slipped and slid trying to stop. Jumbo Joe bolted the ATV across the volcano, drifting and spinning in a way that wasn't controlled, though was intentional. The boar got turned around again.

"You can't catch me! You catch me and I'll rip my arm off and feed it to you myself! You fucking pylon!"

The boar was already charging. Lumpy grey gunk streamed from the beast's snout and eyes, as well as from two wounds to its forehead. It breathed heavily, grunting and growling as it sprinted, hooves clopping like a scene from the Washington Irving comedy about a goofy teacher and a horrific prank played on him.

Jumbo Joe fired, pulled the bolt, fired, pulled the bolt—*click*. He slammed his foot on the accelerator earlier than before, giving the boar a moment to recalibrate, though it did little good. The beast had no immediate way of slowing and Jumbo Joe was already well past him, forcing the boar to skid and slide.

Jumbo Joe put the rifle in the small bed behind the seats and withdrew the handgun from the front pocket of his linen shorts. The boar was already breaking toward him.

"All the marbles here in sudden death overtime," Jumbo Joe said in a rush. He aimed and fired five quick shots into the boar's face, slowing the beast but a hair. "*Next thing you know, shawty got low, low—*" He fired six rapid shots at the boar's feet, tearing its hooves to shreds.

The beast pitched forward, skidding as if on glass until nailing the lip of the volcano and launching into the trees. Jumbo Joe worked quickly, pocketing the handgun and filling the magazine of the rifle.

Armed and ready to dance with danger, Jumbo Joe rolled to the edge of the volcano before hopping out of the ATV to get a look over the edge. The boar had a palm tree driving up through its abdomen and was still trying to rise. Much of the fun and all of the competition drained from the situation.

"Can't leave an animal in pain, Joey," he said, his voice low to mimic the ideal his father had instilled in him as a boy.

He rushed down the hill, slipping in the dirt now and then, but keeping upright. He cast a glance back toward the hotel and was amazed to see how much of the forest had lit already, meaning he had to get his butt moving if he was indeed ever going to make it to a survivor's afterparty.

The boar was on its side, useless though unaware of the fact. It snapped and snorted at Jumbo Joe. Wisely, man kept five feet between himself and the beast's mouth.

"Like potting an empty netter," Jumbo Joe said, aiming in a way that he hoped would pop the boar's cranium, letting its active brain out to die.

It took three rounds before the skull opened and the brain slipped free like Jell-O from a buffet plate. Jumbo Joe took another wee toot from his fingertips, then recalled any number of pigs might be on their way and rushed back up to the volcano. He'd noticed obvious drag marks leading to a shadowy space and had an idea that he was about to do a little spelunking.

29

Mary had found a binder beneath her seat and now it lay open on her lap, flipping through, ready to look up anything Q might've been confused about. He wasn't at all confused, though took a few moments to find switches at times.

"Should I blow the horn a couple times to be sure there's nobody out there?" Q said.

"Better not."

Q nodded. "Hope those piggies fry," he said as he pulled a joint and lighter from his breast pocket.

"Are you sure you should?" Mary said, eyebrows about as high up as they could go.

"Shrooms are all worn off now. Say, do you think you could fix us some coffee? I figure I better stay right here."

Mary nodded.

"If there's still some in the pot, maybe just find me some ice cubes and a little cream." Q took a drag, watching the reflected flicker of the firelight play off the curved windshield. The trip, financially, was a massive L, but in an experience sense, it was invaluable. Drug lords weren't usually impressed by much, but this story would be something to tell.

"Q?" Mary said from the passenger area.

"Yeah?"

"Come here."

Q sighed, putting the burning joint back between his lips so he could use his hands to push himself out of the snug captain's chair. He stepped back into the passenger area—there was no first class seating on the plane as all the seats reclined, had dividers, and plenty of leg room; Jabali Island was not for the working class.

"Look," Mary said, pointing through the open door.

Clopping slowly toward the plane was a pig, smoke rising from its singed hide.

"I didn't figure we were out of this yet. At least there's only one."

Mary snatched the joint from Q's mouth, took a drag, then held her breath as she said, "Only one, *for now*."

30

Jumbo Joe leaned over the hole in the igneous rock that filled the volcano mouth like the foil on a pudding cup. The hole was about the size of a Fiat 500, perhaps a Chrysler Neon. He shined the flashlight attached beneath the barrel of his rifle down. The fall was only about eight feet, but he'd need a way up. He looked around, wishing the ATV had a winch.

"Hmm," he hummed, hurrying around to the back of the ATV. The bed was a dumper, so he pulled the pin and worked the lever to reveal what lay below. A flare. A first-aid kit. Twenty feet of cheap nylon rope. "That'll do."

Jumbo Joe moved the ATV after withdrawing the rope and closing the dumper bed, parking its nose a few inches from the edge of the hole. He stood a moment trying to recall a good knot—fancy knots were not often tested in a farmstead curriculum and Boy Scouts was for city kids who didn't act as slave labor on the family farm. In the end, he tied four overlapping starting knots that bowed inexpertly outward like cysts growing upon cysts but would have to do.

The rifle dropped. Jumbo Joe lowered himself a touch more gracefully, though wasted little time getting it done. It was pitch black down there, the ground beneath the hole was soft and mucky, blood mixed with dirt. The stench was rotten, forcing Jumbo Joe to breathe from his mouth.

With timid steps, he pushed onward. The

space was eerie, and cooler than the atmosphere beyond the volcano. The light beam from the flashlight taped beneath the rifle gave Jumbo Joe an idea of the space, though gave him little for clues concerning just what in the hell was going on down here. He spun a full revolution and caught something sparkly with his beam, then chased after it.

"What in the fuck?" he said, the fingers of his left hand trailing to his pocket and the cocaine therein. The powdered fingers went into his nostrils, and he snuffed back hard. The coke didn't modify what he was looking at.

On the wall before him was a woman, spattered in lumpy grey stuff. The grey stuff was like glue...and looked to be the same stuff coming out of the pigs. Jumbo Joe scanned his mental databanks for something similar in the natural world and found nothing. He shined the beam off the woman. There was a man a couple feet to her left, spattered equally, though his eyes were open and milky. His forehead bulged oddly. Grey gunk was slipping out of his nose in a fat dribble that ran to his lip. The man licked at it absently.

"You alive?" Jumbo Joe whispered. "Or is it just your body?"

The man said nothing, simply stared blankly at Jumbo Joe. It hardly mattered, he wasn't here for this man, not any man for that matter. Wasn't here for that woman either, not here for any woman, not really. He'd worked decades toward earning a goddamned Cup ring and he wasn't about to lose it at some damned ritzy resort full of assholes.

He started moving more quickly around the room. The floor was mostly smooth and free of obstructions. Men and women were hung on the walls, most had their eyes closed, but some had them open, revealing milky globes that looked blind. The waking people seemed almost zombified, though not ravenous or driven, like the pigs.

"Not yet," he whispered, the words echoing around the room.

He kept going. He had to find Susan and hope like hell the ring was still on her thumb—he also had to get her out if she was alive. He liked her, and if he came back with just the ring…

Jumbo Joe picked up the pace, scanning the faces, only vaguely wondering now how these people got stuck to the wall. It appeared three-quarters of all the guests were here, the other quarter were almost certainly dead.

He finally found Susan near the edge of a cave. Her eyes were closed, her body all but lifeless. Her hands were covered in goop. He didn't want to touch the stuff, so he took off his shirt and wiped at it, like mopping up spilled engine oil from a cement floor. It sloughed off her in grey heaps of putrescence, making him think of the anal gland discharge the time a heifer caught something called hemorrhagic bowel syndrome; white, lumpy, unbelievably rank in scent. Enough of the stuff was off Susan after the third swipe that she tumbled to the ground.

Jumbo Joe toed Susan onto her back. Her hands were clearly free of his ring.

"Well, shit, shit, shit!" he said, the words bouncing around him in a reverberated chorus of anger.

He set his rifle down so the light pointed in the direction of the hole. By Susan's feet, he dragged the unconscious woman toward the dangling rope. Leaving the rifle behind made him paranoid, so when he reached the hole, he whipped the handgun from his pocket like a wannabe gunslinger. He scanned the darkness and saw no boogeymen or beasts or anything that seemed apt to jump out and get him.

By four belt loops at the back of Susan's shorts, Jumbo Joe tied her to the ATV. The plan now was to find his ring, climb the rope, and reel her up gingerly. Almost blinded by the light pointed at him and the darkness everywhere else, Jumbo Joe stepped slowly, the handgun out before him, the other hand stretched to feel the emptiness. Once to the rifle, he pocketed the handgun and took hold of the bigger weapon.

Moving faster now, feeling as if he was getting away with something he shouldn't, he scanned the floor of the cavern. After five minutes, he'd made two loops. The diamonds in the ring would sparkle and the gold would reflect.

"Damned thing," he whispered, knowing he'd have to go into the cave, knowing too that whatever had done this to all the resort's guests would be in that cave as well.

Slowly, slowly, slow—Jumbo Joe burst forward into thick darkness upon seeing a telltale sparkle. He bent, snatching up the bulky ring. It went onto his finger, and he sighed in relief. An odd rubbing noise sounded from before him. He lifted the rifle, shining the beam on a six-foot-tall mushroom with a grey cap that was spotted with oblong purple blobs.

"Weird," he whispered, walking backward.

The stem of the mushroom began to open from beneath the cap. One, two, three…eight long legs. The mushroom turned and Jumbo Joe saw the face of a spider, its proboscis dripping grey sludge.

"Fuck no," he said, firing three quick rounds into the thing. It pitched sideways, then dropped. "Huh."

There was movement in the darkness. A mushroom nearly twice the size was lumbering up from a sitting position. Jumbo Joe didn't wait for it to get all the way to its feet before he spun on his heels and broke for the opening and the rope and Susan's prone body.

He unbuttoned his shorts and stuffed the rifle down. The skinny rope wasn't easy to climb, but Jumbo Joe's upper body strength had never failed him before and it didn't now. Topside, the rifle came out of his shorts, he rebuttoned, and he burned it to the ATV's driver's seat. From within the volcano, he heard the undeniable scratching of an impossible spider chasing after him.

"Sorry, Susan," he said a moment before hitting the accelerator pedal and rocketing the ATV forward, whipping Susan out of the hole.

Jumbo Joe winced watching her bounce, slamming on the brakes when she was about eight feet past the hole. He reversed until he was almost on top of her, then hopped off the ATV and ran around back to pop her in the dumper bed. Thankfully, she couldn't have weighed more than 135 pounds.

The bigger spider's legs appeared topside as Jumbo Joe raced back to the driver's seat, laughing to himself over the insanity of Jabali Island. Smoke now filled the atmosphere, as did the scent of cooked meat.

"Nice try, you can't stop Jumbo Motherfucking…" Jumbo Joe trailed, his mind shifting from rooster crowing to outracing a fire that seemed twice as driven and hungry as any of the oversized piggies had.

Trees toppled and the forest floor itself danced with flames. He put his foot down, rocking and bouncing. Unwilling to let go of the rifle, he reached between the seats to the bed and pinched Susan down with the deadly steel.

Jumbo Joe ducked—despite being within a roll cage—and yanked the wheel left when a tree to his right toppled above him. The heat had him slick, oozing sweat from scalp to toenails. He squinted at the brightness as he aimed for the beach, praying the rubber of the tires didn't blow, then light—not much burned better once it got going than some Goodyears.

It became too much and Jumbo Joe closed his eyes, foot pinned to the accelerator. He could only hope he didn't wreck. The smoke became too thick then and as well as not seeing, he quit breathing. Soon he'd be dead or on the beach.

Then it happened and comparatively cool air consumed him. He gasped. His eyes opened. He jerked the wheel to keep from driving into the ocean.

"I won, you scummy fucking insect!" he shouted, almost howling to the ever-lightening sky of early, early morning.

31

The queen spider climbed up from beneath the solidified lava through the hole and stretched to its full height of sixteen feet. With its many eyes, it watched Jumbo Joe's ATV cut through the burning forest, heading toward the beach.

There was little time to waste; the spider would conquer and enslave this threat as it had the pigs. This was the only way to ensure safety and survival.

The spider crossed the volcano and climbed down to the far side. It started toward the section of beach that had not yet been molested by the resort's reach. Feeling the heat, the spider began to sprint, its long legs moving in a haze like images in a zoetrope.

Jabali Island belonged to the queen spider, and this queen spider refused to let the human threat continue, not while her egg sac back in the volcano inched toward maturity.

32

Mary raced back to the plane after sprinting to grab the rifle that had gone flying in the ATV snafu. She charged up the rolling staircase and dropped flat to her tummy. Two pigs had made it out of the blazing forest and to the runway. Both seemed discombobulated, uncertain of their task; neither had noticed the frantic play to grab the rifle. At first, it felt okay that they were out there and up to very little, but Q reminded her it wouldn't take much to make a plane unflyable.

She aimed through both sights, waiting for the pigs to draw near enough that the shots might make a difference; if the pigs went elsewhere, that was fine too. Though, there wasn't a great deal of elsewhere remaining on Jabali Island. Everything but the sand and the runway appeared to be on fire.

Q remained in the cockpit drinking cold coffee, eating individually wrapped cookies, and smoking weed. He'd tried the radio a few times and found it useless; none of the voices that he'd reached spoke a lick of English. Still, he explained the situation on the island, hoping someone would be recording, then replaying said recording to an English ear. It wasn't as if anyone could come help them. It was simply too late for that—the flight from Santiago Airport to Jabali Island was more than six hours. He guessed it was possible someone could get there much sooner if departing from Easter Island, but whom? Easter Island wasn't a mecca of emergency services, nor of civilization, nor of up-to-date technologies. It was an island in the middle of nowhere, its only draw was strange monoliths.

He'd radio in once he was close to the mainland while preparing to descend. Thankfully, it was wildly easy to flip a past flight plan in the plane's system, creating a return route. Once in the air, all they'd have to worry about was flying where they shouldn't, once they were over busier airspace.

A muffled shot rang out. Q rose from his seat and hurried through the cabin door, the attendants' station, and finally to the jetway door. Mary remained where she was, watching the two pigs milling about.

"You hit one?" Q said, standing over the sprawled woman.

"No. Something blew over near where the hotel had been."

"Ah," Q said, then broached the subject they'd both been avoiding. "How long do we wait before we give up on Mr. Hockey Man?"

Mary sighed. "I don't know. A wee bit yet, I should think."

Smoke began to settle like a fog, pushing the pigs closer. The sun would come up in the next hour and a half, and they couldn't be on the island when it did. By then, it would simply be too hot and too smoky to take off safely, if the engine didn't cut out.

"A wee bit like five minutes?"

Before Mary could answer, one of the pigs trotted toward the staircase. She took aim, waiting for the beast to get close, close, close enough.

"If you're going to shoot, shoot it on this side. We won't be able to—"

Mary fired, silencing Q's direction. The shot hit the pig in its face, plowing through bone, meat, and grey sludge. When the pig dropped, it dropped heavily enough that what remained of its brain spewed out from the round's exit hole.

"Bullseye," Mary said. "One to go. It comes anywhere near—"

It was Q's turn to cut her off. "Look at the beach."

A pair of lights played alongside the ocean. An ATV.

"Shit."

Mary pulled the bolt and chambered a fresh round. She fired at the other pig, which was about thirty yards from the plane. The round hit the pig a foot from the base of its tail. It turned and sniffed.

"Get its attention," Mary said.

Q sighed, then began jumping and waving his arms above his head. "All right. Soowee! Soowee! Piggy, piggy! Here, piggy, piggy!"

The pig started toward them in a hurry, making it almost as close as the other pig had before yanking its head sideways to face the ATV racing across the runway.

"Shit," Mary said, then took the shot anyway.

The pig began to run toward the ATV, creating distance and decreasing the chances of nailing a clean and deadly hit.

"That ain't good," Q said. "I'll be in the cabin." He broke away, leaving Mary on the floor.

Mary pulled the bolt, chambered a fresh round, then fired.

33

Jumbo Joe could see the runway and hooted into the night, fist-pumping like he'd just potted an OT winner. The ATV had no mirrors, but he had no interest in looking back. Forward was a future; forward was his way off this pig-infested island.

As he drew closer, his focus zeroed in on the rolling staircase. He saw someone lying flat with a rifle pointed. This got him looking around. Then he spotted it, only ten feet away, a goddamned pig. It was charging him. Jumbo Joe jerked the wheel away. The pig leapt, turning with him.

It was directly behind him, but the ATV was faster, quickly making distance—the lights of the dash flashed and the scent of burnt plastic puffed up in a noxious cloud. The pig was almost on them as the ATV rocked to a stop; something integral had obviously melted.

"Sheee-it!" Jumbo Joe said, launching himself off the ATV the same moment a shot rang out.

The pig dropped, skidding on its belly, legs splayed out sideways. The beast attempted to rise, but one leg was shattered, rendered useless by Mary's sharp shooting.

"Ha! Nice try, piggy!"

The pig attempted to crawl, snapping its jaws as it did so. Jumbo Joe ignored it and hurried back to the ATV. He popped the shifter into neutral and began to push, jogging alongside the vehicle, moving easily upon the smooth runway. It took a little more than a minute for him to reach the stairs.

"Did you get her?" Mary said from the top of the stairs.

"Sure," Jumbo Joe said, as if it was a simple day at the rink. "Grab a blanket, she's covered in that grey gunk."

The plane's engines came to life with a smooth, trustworthy rumble.

Mary disappeared and reappeared mere seconds later. She pitched a blanket at Jumbo Joe and carried a second blanket as she hurried down to the tarmac. They wiped furiously, Susan's body limp and doll-like in their hands.

"What is this stuff?" Mary said, almost yelling to be heard.

"There's weirder shit on this island than giant pigs!" Jumbo Joe said, picking up a cocooned Susan as if she were a feed bag, jerking her onto a shoulder. "Tell you in the air! Grab my rifle."

Mary coughed as she bent for the weapon. The smoke had now settled on the tarmac like a fog, making the forest and everything beyond all but invisible. "She's breathing at least."

Jumbo Joe led the parade up the stairs, the steel rickety beneath him—the system hadn't been latched onto the plane. Mary was right behind him, looking back. Dragging itself along the runway was the pig with the shot leg.

"Damned place," she whispered before stepping into the plane, pulling the door to the mid-way point behind her. She looked over her shoulder to where Jumbo Joe was buckling Susan's unconscious form into a seat. "Can you push away the ladder so I can close the door?"

"Sure," Jumbo Joe said as he finished leaning Susan's seat back so she wouldn't slouch forward.

Q popped out of the cockpit. "Man, we gotta go. Close that door."

"On it," Mary said.

Jumbo Joe, from his knees, pushed the stairs away far enough to seal the door. The quiet was immediate and welcome. The cabin air was already pumping stuff fresher than what was outside. Jumbo Joe rose, looked left, then right, and once spotting it, headed for the kitchen area. The plane lurched beneath them.

"What are you doing?" Mary said, jogging to catch up, both rifles in her hands.

"Just wetting my whistle." Jumbo Joe opened a fridge and with one hand pulled out four bottles of Heineken. He then opened a cupboard and located a box of individually wrapped cookies. "Remember when you could have nuts on a plane, before *everyone* suddenly became allergic?"

"Yes, well, you can usually acquire nuts in first class…though this whole plane is at least business class."

"I don't care if it's no class, as long as we get off this damned island."

The plane began a turn, rocking Jumbo Joe

and Mary. Mary slunk sideways through the aisle to the cabin door. Jumbo Joe trailed behind her.

They opened the cabin door and a billow of smoke poured out. Mary coughed and Jumbo Joe groaned—then, as if unrelated, thought he might like an upper from his back pocket.

Mary sat shotgun and Jumbo Joe plunked down on the third seat, his legs stretching across the cockpit. He set aside his meal, leaning forward as he did so. With access, he retrieved the coke baggy from his pocket, forcing himself to abstain; the shit was wonderful, too wonderful.

"Hey," he said, holding the torn, dusty baggy out to Mary. "Better take that in case he comes down or whatever happens after all that weed."

Mary took the baggy with gentle, almost fearful hands. Q was too busy focusing on the task. They were at the end of the runway and looking out at a smoky wall.

"If anything's in our path on the runway now, we're all dead," Q said, then began accelerating.

Jumbo Joe popped a beer on a steel ledge for Mary, then one for himself, absently slipping the bent caps into his pocket. Mary took a mouthful while Jumbo Joe crushed the entire bottle, his large Adam's apple bouncing fives time in total until all that remained was the foamy ghost of suds past. He cracked another just as the plane left the tarmac. They rose at the typical speed, but it felt like forever, as if they'd never reach cruising altitude. Then it happened, they were flying smoothly, away from Jabali Island and its freakish inhabitants.

Something knocked heavily from beyond the cockpit, feeling as if it rocked the entire plane. Q looked to Mary. Mary looked to Jumbo Joe.

"Is that coming from an engine?" Jumbo Joe said.

"Doesn't appear that way. Go check if you can see something out the window. I totally neglected routine prior to take-off." Q had his focus forward when he spoke.

The biggest thump yet rattled through them. Jumbo Joe finished his second beer, then stood. He exited the cabin and was gone only a handful of seconds before returning.

"Remember when I told you I'd tell you about the weirder shit than the pigs?"

Mary nodded, her jaw slack.

"So, there's this enormous spider and I kind of killed its buddy, or partner, or offspring and now it's on the side of the plane, trying…"

The spider slammed its feet against the thick exterior steel.

"…to break in."

"What'll we do?" Mary said.

"Something," Jumbo Joe said.

Q shot a look at Jumbo Joe, then straightened; something was hitting him, and his expression changed. He pointed to the binder between the captains' seats. "Mary, darling, be a dear and look up depressurizing the cabin. If we get a hole while we're flying, we'll likely blow to bits."

Mary grabbed the binder and flipped to the

index.

34

Things didn't look good. Mary held her breath as she left the cockpit to inspect the spider through a window. At first, while banging its sturdy legs against the hull, it appeared it might slip off and they'd be done with it. It eventually got a grip, straddling the underside of the plane, legs wrapped around either wing. If it stayed that way, they likely could've waited. But now, the damned thing was pawing at an engine.

After a glance at Susan, who remained asleep amid a sea of dangling plastic vines, one of the masks at the end of those vines attached to her face, Mary broke back to the cockpit, forcing open the now heavy door. There was oxygen but it felt thinner than normal in the still pressurized cabin. Mary took a deep, moderately satisfying breath.

Jumbo Joe was leaned over the rifle and the handgun. Q was at the helm. Mary skirted Jumbo Joe and the weaponry and fell into the co-pilot's chair.

"It's going for an engine. What happens if it—"

"I'm on it," Jumbo Joe said. They had two rifle rounds and nine more bullets for the handgun.

"How?" Mary said.

"According to that binder, there are escape ropes for if the plane crashes somewhere soft enough that anybody survives. I'm going to use those ropes and go out there, end that damned spider like a buzzer beater."

Q laughed, reaching across the dash for the open baggy—they'd all been tooting now to keep focus on the task before them. "Guess you'll need some turbo courage."

Jumbo Joe nodded. "I'll be back."

He forced through the heavy door and hurried to the storage area he'd read about in the binder. He found the ropes, as well as a deflated life raft in a canvas duffel bag. Upon removing the bag and the ropes, he discovered a large ring with two-dozen stainless-steel carabiners attached. He grabbed those as well and hurried back to the cabin.

Mary, having spent a decent chunk of time in her youth on sailing vessels—her schools always had teams—tied the knots after Jumbo Joe decided where he needed the ropes. The rope would be tied off inside the plane, directly across from the door to the world beyond.

"What are you doing with the raft?" Mary said.

"Don't know," Jumbo Joe said, studying a carabiner. "Either of you ever see that movie, *Cliffhanger*?"

Mary shook her head.

"Totally dumb," Q said.

"Not as dumb as this." Jumbo Joe dropped the extra carabiners and reached for the cocaine baggy. He put his nose into the opening, then inhaled as deeply as possible. Naturally, his head jerked back. His nose and upper lip were powdered white.

"Let's go!" he shouted, stuffing the handgun in his pocket, then grabbing the raft and the rifle with his other hands. "Let's do it, baby!"

Jumbo Joe burst through the unlatched cockpit door like the Kool-Aid man—Mary hurried out after him to tie off the rope as he spun the handle to the jetway door. Mary tapped his shoulder once done and raced back to the cabin for a semblance of safety.

The door swung open. Jumbo Joe wore the raft duffel bag like a backpack and had the rifle in his hands. The spider had stretched itself to the near wing, attempting to spray that chunky grey goop into the engine. It seemed more luck than intelligence that the creature was after something that could take the plane down.

Jumbo Joe leapt out and was yanked hard enough sideways that he spun, the rifle launching from his hands. He tried to gasp and couldn't until he cupped his hands around his nose and mouth. Once he regained some of his mental equilibrium, he recognized that the spider was looking back at him. He was about three feet behind the spider, and likely could've shot into its abdomen, but the angle was all wrong and the shots very well might go into the plane itself, causing who knew what damage.

He pressed his feet firmly against the bottom of the plane and was now standing upside down. He withdrew the handgun from his pocket and attempted to leap like a skydiver. The wind was too great, sending him flat against the hull and rattling his teeth together. He felt pebbly crumbs on his tongue. He already had three implants up front and would need some more dental work if he ever got out of this.

Against the wind, he got himself upright again, the soles of his shoes firm against the hull. He looked at the spider. It had turned and was now facing him fully, looking ready to pounce. He cupped his empty hand over his mouth to take a breath, accidentally blocking the flow of grey goop exiting the spider's outstretched proboscis. The stuff was warm and felt alive, tiny organisms dancing upon his flesh, looking for a way inside.

"Ek!" Jumbo Joe said, panicking, swiping at the stuff. The handgun, slick with gunk, flew from his grip.

The spider unloaded a fresh helping of sludge and Jumbo Joe ducked below the nasty deluge. While hunched forward, the release cord of the life raft dangled before him.

"All right, toughy!" he shouted and began reeling in the rope attaching him to the plane. He quickly closed the distance between him and the spider. He felt the spider, felt the goop ooze over his shirtless shoulders. "Sudden death time, bay-bee!"

Jumbo Joe closed his eyes and pulled the release cord and was immediately whipped away from the plane. When he looked, the plane was spider-less.

"Got you, you—"

The spider's face leaned over Jumbo Joe's back as he sailed in the blasting sky beneath the plane. Grey gunk began oozing and spraying, coating Jumbo Joe. He zipped his lips tight and shook his head like a kid refusing to eat their greens. The hairy feet of the spider started down his chest, as if seeking an opening. Jumbo Joe attempted to pull the straps of the duffel bag far enough that he might get a shoulder out, but the pressure pushing against the huge raft refused him.

The grey gunk slid across his face as if actively seeking his sinus. He continued shaking his head and pulling on the straps. The spider's feet dipped lower, one sliding inside his shorts. Jumbo Joe screamed shrilly at this, feeling a bottle cap in his pocket grind against his thigh.

Here was hope.

Jumbo Joe forgot the spider and all its unwanted passes at trying to swap saliva and get into his drawers. He pulled the pinched cap from his pocket. He grabbed at the thick rubber of the raft and began sawing. The spider continued its body cavity search, that leg in his shorts dipping down, pinching his balls on the way back up.

Jumbo Joe kept shaking and sawing at the rubber raft until a hole formed. He inserted a finger and tore. The rip was long and satisfying. The raft lost shape and began flapping like a parachute with crossed lines. Jumbo Joe pulled the straps away from his chest and got one arm free. The raft shot off his back, taking with it the spider.

For three minutes, Jumbo Joe dangled beneath the plane, cupping his face, trying to catch his breath. By and by, he calmed, and once capable, began reeling himself in, winding the rope around his right arm as he did so.

35

"Holy shit, you're alive," Q said, laughing.

Jumbo Joe was red all over from the wind and had a skein of grey film upon his face and chest—most of the gunk had blown away. He fell into the third seat and reached for a beer.

"Repressurize, I need to take a sink bath. That spider was getting a little fresh."

"It's gone?" Mary said, expression stretched wide as was possible.

"Gone as Dutton's Curse," Jumbo Joe said, then emptied his beer.

"What is Dutton's Curse?" Mary grabbed the binder as she spoke.

Jumbo Joe waved this question off—almost certainly neither cared about the Rangers' Cup drought that ran from 1940 to 1994, or that the New York Americans never got back into the NHL.

The air became more normal almost instantly, and within a few minutes, the cockpit door opened smoothly, and they went back to remove Susan's oxygen mask. She was still asleep.

Jumbo Joe stripped naked and bathed himself with the washroom door open—there was simply no room to get to everything with his entire body inside. He put what little clothes he had back on and dropped down into the row of seats across from Susan. He leaned back and closed his eyes. They were going to make it, sure, but he was out of a job once again.

"Eighteen years straight of pro paychecks and I lose two jobs in six months," he said to himself. He was crashing hard, but doubted the coke would let him sleep. He considered returning to the cockpit, ask Q for some weed to help him sleep, but decided against it. In a sea halfway between waking and sleep, Jumbo Joe rocked, brain all but quiet.

After more than an hour since knocking the spider away, Jumbo Joe reached for the TV and scrolled through the few dozen movie offerings until he reached the flight display. They appeared to be a little better than halfway back to Santiago Airport.

He snapped off the set and sat back again, eyes closed. He wondered what he might do moving forward. He wasn't broke, but life was expensive without work to fill the gaps, and he was only turning thirty-nine in February. He might live fifty more years. The three million he had in the bank account—he'd done his share of unwise gambling in the early part of his career, back when he was paid just shy of eight figures per season, and clearing better than half that after taxes—alongside two cars, a truck, and a mansion wouldn't keep him busy for the next forty, fifty years.

Being a celebrity bouncer at an exclusive resort looked good on paper and in the propaganda videos they'd sent him, and probably it should've been okay. He wouldn't do it again, though he was now thinking a little excitement wouldn't hurt. This job had been rich in excitement. Maybe he'd move to the territories or Alaska, become a celebrity tour guide of sorts, anything and anywhere that gave him a break from pigs and spiders and rich assholes.

He tongued at the molar he'd broken outside the plane. "Dentist first," he said, then amended, "Bed first, then dentist."

36

Susan dreamed of pain. Her head and face felt ready to burst, as if she had too much mucus and too much grey matter. She dreamed of darkness and of motion. She dreamed she'd been taken onboard an alien vessel and was floating through space, the vacuum of the great beyond increasing the pressure on her face.

"…is…our…apt…ee…ill…ee…make…our…sent…into," Susan opened her eyes, hearing the rest as if underwater, "Santiago, Chile, inside ten minutes. Thank you for choosing to fly with Q."

She tried to rise. The belt around her hips was tight. Susan pawed dumbly at the buckle until a memory slid home and she pressed the button that released the coupler. Her legs were wobbly, but she managed to stand. Directly ahead, she heard voices and needed to be with them. The drive was almost too much, the hunger.

Stumbling, her feet shuffling, Susan moved toward the cockpit, passing a reflective glass cupboard panel that mirrored a version of herself she likely wouldn't have recognized right away. In the last forty minutes or so, the spider's medicine had cured her of a sturdy skull, cured her of the mundane worries of a human, and cured her of all but a hint of her past self.

The cockpit door was open a crack and she pulled it the rest of the way.

"Probably be wise to flush the rest of the coke down the toilet before we land," Q said, eyes forward.

“Right,” Mary said, grabbing the depleted baggy and rising, turning, seeing the mutated Susan standing before her.

37

Mary shrieked when Susan's hands came up to grab her by the shoulders and reel her in. Susan's mouth was stretched wide and aimed at Mary's throat.

"What in the fuck is going on?" Q said, the words tumbling out of him.

Mary, coke baggy in hand, tried to wrestle herself free. The coke dropped to the floor, a powdery puff flaring out in a tiny mushroom cloud.

Susan's mouth planted against Mary's throat, her teeth raking the flesh. A fresh dose of adrenaline surged through Mary, and she flung the less than stable woman backward. Susan, once done moving in reverse, charged forward.

Mary held the woman at arm's length. "No! No!" she shouted.

Then it came at her like a 3D gimmick from an '80s slasher. Mary shrieked again, a goo-covered fist stopping an inch from her nose, grey gunk splattered about her face. Jumbo Joe pulled his hand back as Susan fell, lifeless, the rest of her skull giving way into a puddle of gore. Jumbo Joe hopped in reverse and the woman's body came to rest on the carpet, covering the cocaine.

Mary stood in shock, taking short and frantic sips of breath, her arms out before her, her fingers spread wide.

"Damn well should've left her," Jumbo Joe said, leaning down to appreciate the destruction his fist had caused. Everything from Susan's eyebrows up was a mucky, mushy mess. "I guess—"

Q spoke, and loudly, into his headset. "This is going to sound crazy, but…"

Jumbo Joe quit listening and began dragging Susan's corpse out of the cockpit doorway. The coke was there, much of it ground into the carpet. Mary, since she was heading to the can anyway, scooped up what she could and started away.

Q continued telling their story to the Chilean controllers on the ground. Once Susan was removed, Jumbo Joe took up his seat behind the co-pilot's chair. From the floor, he grabbed six individually wrapped cookies and began to eat.

—

Satellite imagery confirmed the fire on the island. The public was already made aware of a *hoax* of at least one psychotic pig at the exclusive Jabali Resort, thanks to an Instagram post made by a one Summer Dallas who spotted a beast, attempted to pet it, and was devoured just off-camera.

The trio of survivors were kept in quarantine for seventy-two hours. The body of Susan Marshall disappeared into the hands of governmental scientists. Nobody seemed to buy that a spider had somehow enlarged and zombified a pack of pigs and took all the resort's guests hostage with aims of enslaving the humans. Unfortunately for those grilling the trio, their stories never changed. None admitted to their heavy drug use, but it hardly seemed pertinent.

"Some vacation, huh?" Mary said, dressed in nurse's scrubs.

She, Jumbo Joe, and Q had all been released from a private wing of a large, industrious hospital, and were awaiting their rides. Mary was being picked up by the British consulate, who would arrange her travel back to England. Jumbo Joe was waiting on a cab to take him to the Canadian consulate.

"This is me," Q said as a long, black limousine with government tags on the plate pulled to the curb. "Nice knowing you, Mary. Jumbo Joe, you go easy on the white horse, she can be a wild one…you fucking prick." He winked.

Jumbo Joe opened his mouth to rebut but closed it without speaking.

Directly behind the limo was Mary's ride—a respectable Mercedes, but no limousine. She offered Jumbo Joe a nod and said, "Well, that certainly was interesting."

"No doubt," Jumbo Joe said.

"Cheers," Mary said, nodding again before climbing into the car.

Suddenly, he was alone, back in civilization and among scores of people, with no prospects for his future. He began to run through the jobs he'd be willing to do and sighed. He'd tried to fight it, as it felt like a cliché, but he guessed he could become a high-profile personal trainer, like so many other guys in his position.

"Has-beens," he whispered to himself and closed his eyes.

He sat like that for less than a minute before a voice shouted, "Bro! Dude, it's fucking Jumbo Joe!"

Jumbo Joe opened his eyes to two young men with zinc on their noses. They each wore an oversized Panama hat, linen shorts, flip-flops, and hockey jerseys—one a Nordiques jersey and the other an Ice Gators jersey. They had on big smiles and hands out with cellphones in their grips.

"Can we get a selfie?" one said.

"Sure thing," Jumbo Joe said and took both men in loose headlocks.

They each snapped a shot, checked the results, then snapped a couple more. Quickly, each regaled Jumbo Joe with their favorite of his past actions on the ice, then asked for autographs before hurrying into the airport to catch a flight back to America.

Alone again, Jumbo Joe Bourque, Cup ring sparkling on his right hand, began to whistle an old Stompin' Tom Connors tune while he awaited his ride.

THE END

Check out other great

Cryptid Novels!

J.H. Moncrieff

RETURN TO DYATLOV PASS

In 1959, nine Russian students set off on a skiing expedition in the Ural Mountains. Their mutilated bodies were discovered weeks later. Their bizarre and unexplained deaths are one of the most enduring true mysteries of our time. Nearly sixty years later, podcast host Nat McPherson ventures into the same mountains with her team, determined to finally solve the mystery of the Dyatlov Pass incident. Her plans are thwarted on the first night, when two trackers from her group are brutally slaughtered. The team's guide, a superstitious man from a neighboring village, blames the killings on yetis, but no one believes him. As members of Nat's team die one by one, she must figure out if there's a murderer in their midst—or something even worse—before history repeats itself and her group becomes another casualty of the infamous Dead Mountain.

Gerry Griffiths

CRYPTID ZOO

As a child, rare and unusual animals, especially cryptid creatures, always fascinated Carter Wilde. Now that he's an eccentric billionaire and runs the largest conglomerate of high-tech companies all over the world, he can finally achieve his wildest dream of building the most incredible theme park ever conceived on the planet... CRYPTID ZOO. Even though there have been apparent problems with the project, Wilde still decides to send some of his marketing employees and their families on a forced vacation to assess the theme park in preparation for Opening Day. Nick Wells and his family are some of those chosen and are about to embark on what will become the most terror-filled weekend of their lives—praying they survive. STEP RIGHT UP AND GET YOUR FREE PASS... TO CRYPTID ZOO

Check out other great

Cryptid Novels!

Hunter Shea

THE DOVER DEMON

The Dover Demon is real...and it has returned. In 1977, Sam Brogna and his friends came upon a terrifying, alien creature on a deserted country road. What they witnessed was so bizarre, so chilling, they swore their silence. But their lives were changed forever. Decades later, the town of Dover has been hit by a massive blizzard. Sam's son, Nicky, is drawn to search for the infamous cryptid, only to disappear into the bowels of a secret underground lair. The Dover Demon is far deadlier than anyone could have believed. And there are many of them. Can Sam and his reunited friends rescue Nicky and battle a race of creatures so powerful, so sinister, that history itself has been shaped by their secretive presence? "THE DOVER DEMON is Shea's most delightful and insidiously terrifying monster yet." – Shotgun Logic Reviews "An excellent horror novel and a strong standout in the UFO and cryptid subgenres." –Hellnotes "Non-stop action awaits those brave enough to dive into the small town of Dover, and if you're lucky, you won't see the Demon himself!" – The Scary Reviews PRAISE FOR SWAMP MONSTER MASSACRE "B-horror movie fans rejoice, Hunter Shea is here to bring you the ultimate tale of terror!" – Horror Novel Reviews "A nonstop thrill ride! I couldn't put this book down." – Cedar Hollow Horror Reviews

Armand Rosamilia

THE BEAST

The end of summer, 1986. With only a few days left until the new school year, twins Jeremy and Jack Schaffer are on very different paths. Jeremy is the geek, playing Dungeons & Dragons with friends Kathleen and Randy, while Jack is the jock, getting into trouble with his buddies. And then everything changes when neighbor Mister Higgins is killed by a wild animal in his yard. Was it a bear? There's something big lurking in the woods behind their New Jersey home.Will the police be able to solve the murder before more Middletown residents are ripped apart?

www.ingramcontent.com/pod-product-compliance
Lightning Source LLC
Chambersburg PA
CBHW072239190626
46809CB00018B/2853

* 9 7 8 1 9 2 2 8 6 1 9 7 9 *